WALTZING WITH HARRY

"Could you not have picked a less conspicuous place to contact me?" Francie whispered fiercely, as she placed her hand in Ransome's and allowed herself to be led out onto the dance floor. "I hope you realize I shall now become the rage overnight, and all because of you. Worse, it will undoubtedly be all over Town by tomorrow morning that you and I are—are . . . I mean that you have . . ."

"Singled you out for my attentions?" Harry finished for her. "Is the notion so very distasteful to you, Lady Powell?" he queried mildly, as, her hand in his, he swung her around to face him.

Francie's heart leaped as she felt his firm arm slip lightly around her waist. Indeed, she had the most peculiar sensation of having just run a foot race as she felt her pulse, not to mention her respiration, rapidly accelerating beyond the normal rate. Worse, she seemed to have lost the ability to think with any coherence.

It had never occurred to her before that dancing in a man's arms could be so wonderfully blissful. She could no more come up with the words to describe the feelings she was experiencing than she could explain why Ransome should have been the one to generate them . . .

Books by Sara Blayne

PASSION'S LADY
DUEL OF THE HEART
A NOBLEMAN'S BRIDE
AN ELUSIVE GUARDIAN
AN EASTER COURTSHIP
A NOBLE DECEPTION
THEODORA
A NOBLE PURSUIT

Published by Zebra Books

A NOBLE PURSUIT

Sara Blayne

ZEBRA BOOKS
Kensington Publishing Corp.
http://www.zebrabooks.com

ZEBRA BOOKS are published by

Kensington Publishing Corp.
850 Third Avenue
New York, NY 10022

First Printing: September, 1997
10 9 8 7 6 5 4 3 2 1

Printed in the United States of America

*In loving memory of Kathryn A. Hurt,
my mom, whose spirit was as adventurous
as any of my heroines.*

One

Greensward, the Earl of Bancroft's country manor, had never looked so beautiful to Francine Powell as it did that morning viewed from Lathrop Tower. How she loved the Elizabethan house that had been in the Powell family for seven generations! The ivy-covered manor, perched on a low hill in the middle of a sea of green, rolling fields with Bancroft Beck, a purling ribbon flashing silvery through their midst, grew misty in her vision as it came to her how greatly she would miss it. She would miss the carefree days of her girlhood spent in glorious rides on Jester, the thoroughbred stallion she had trained as a green colt; in rough and tumble games with her younger brothers, Timothy and Tom; or in slipping away from her governess (whom she shared with her younger sister Josephine) in order to help her father and brothers with the lambing.

Miss Gladden, the sorely tried governess, had come to despair of ever making a proper lady of the next to the youngest of the earl's four daughters, which suited Francie. She had not the least desire to groom herself for the Marriage Mart. It was not that she had anything against the idea of marriage. Her mama and papa, after all, were a perfect example of just how happy a good marriage could be. And it certainly was not that she disliked men, Francie assured herself. She dearly loved her papa and tolerated her three brothers with the fondness of long familiarity. She adored her sister Lucy's husband Phillip, the Duke of Lathrop, even if he had been instrumental in ruining what Lucy had promised would be Francie's "wondrous, great adventure." She even suspected she could come quite easily to like Paul Moberly, the intriguing, if somewhat elusive Marquis of Leighton her sister Florence had married the previous spring. She might have done, that was, had he not chosen to take himself off almost immediately to Lisbon before anyone, let alone his bride, could really come to know him.

Francie's smooth brow puckered in a frown. How very curious that was, not at all what one would expect of a man who had gone out of his way to court a female in her second Season, one, moreover, whose marriage portion was only a little more than respectable. Not that Leighton had required a wealthy wife. His income and holdings were great enough to make Florence the envy of a host of matchmaking mamas intent on snaring a title and a fortune for their aspiring daughters. He was, in fact, reputed to be rich as Croesus. Furthermore, he was young, only eight and twenty, and while not precisely handsome, was possessed of a strong, manly countenance. Furthermore, a noted Corinthian, he was just the sort who might have had his pick of the eligible young beauties who made their way to London each spring in the hopes of contracting a brilliant match. That he had set his sights on Florence Anne Marie Powell had taken nearly everyone by surprise—everyone, that was, but Florence's mama, who had never once doubted fortune would eventually smile on her second daughter.

Poor Flo. It seemed that nothing had turned out quite the way one might have expected of the undisputed Beauty of the family. As the daughter of the Earl of Bancroft, her connections were impeccable. As the sister of the Duchess of Lathrop, she should have been assured of a *success fou*. The truth was, however, that Flo had not taken at all well, a circumstance which Florence had not hesitated to blame all on Lucy, whom she accused of deliberately going out of her way to make Flo display to disadvantage.

How very like Florence, Francie thought with a wry grimace. And how very absurd. Even as a married woman who had been obviously breeding, it was practically inevitable that Lucy would outshine her younger sister. Besides having red hair and eyes that shone grey-green like the mist on the moors, Lucy was a gifted writer of romance novels. She sparkled with an inner fire and vitality that must draw attention wherever she went.

Lucy kindly had attributed Florence's failure to the possibility that Flo had been rather too nice in her tastes. The truth was, however, that Florence foolishly had set her cap only for the wealthiest, most eligible partis, and had been judged ambitious and overweaning—two qualities that were utterly ruinous for a female in her first Season. In the unenviable position of having to endure a second Season, unattached and tainted by failure, it would have been marvelous indeed had Flo not felt more than a little desperate, Francie mused. A *third* Season, after all, would clearly have been unthinkable. As it was, Flo's second Season had promised fair to be a dismal repetition of the first—until Leighton had fortuitously appeared on the scene and demonstrated what had given every appearance of being an instant *tendre* for Florence.

Indeed, Francie, having struck up an easy camaraderie with Leighton during the days preceding the wedding, had been certain that the marquis's affections for her sister were quite real. Why, then, should he suddenly absent himself from his bride scarcely three months after the ceremony had taken place?

Francie sighed, unable to supply an answer to that intriguing question, especially as Florence stubbornly pretended that absolutely nothing was amiss. Not even Lucy, to whom they all went for sympathy and advice, had been admitted into Flo's confidence. And if Florence had revealed anything to their mama, Lady Emmaline had never chosen to betray so much as a hint of it.

Still, Florence was a married woman now, and since Lady Emmaline had decided that she herself would do better to remain in the country with Josephine, who was prone to colds and inflammations of the throat, it was deemed perfectly acceptable for Flo to bring out her younger sister. Blast the luck!

Francie's life at Greensward, aside from the unavoidable and much loathed piano lessons, tatting, and needlework, suited her perfectly well. She had not the least wish to leave it, especially for a come-out in London, which she viewed as being at the very least a nuisance and at the very most an utter waste of time. After all, if the acknowledged Beauty of the family had proven a failure, what chance had one who felt positively cheated at having been born a female and who was wholly lacking in accomplishments, unless one counted such boyish feats as being able to hurl a rock with unerring accuracy, to climb a tree with the agility of a squirrel, or to ride anything on four legs with a daring that was not only the envy of her brothers, but promised to turn her mama's hair prematurely grey? There was no chance at all that she would make a match, Francie told herself with grim satisfaction, which was just fine with her. She, after all, would prefer to remain just as she was— unattached and therefore free to pursue her own sort of life unfettered by a disapproving husband.

If only she had not to go through the motions of a come-out and all that that would entail, she thought dismally.

Faith, it was bad enough that she would have to give up her breeches and boots and ride sidesaddle, but to be limited to a sedate trot in Hyde Park under the constant supervision of a gooseberry was simply too horrid to contemplate. She might have been somewhat reconciled to so ignominious a fate by the knowledge that Lucy had at least prevailed upon their papa to allow Francie to take Jester with her. She might, that was, had she not to look forward to something so reprehensible as two whole months spent under the aegis of the suffocatingly prim and proper Florence.

"Hell and the devil confound it!" she declared to the tower room at large. "I shall most assuredly end up a murderer or a candidate for Bedlam if I have to listen to Flo prose on about the proprieties every day for an eternity of eight weeks. Oh, why had Lucy to choose now to have her lying in? She has already presented Lathrop with the requisite heir, but now she must go a step further and give him twin daughters when she knows very well she promised to bring me out. Really, it is too bad of Lucy."

"Francine Elizabeth Powell," exclaimed a gently disapproving voice at Francie's back. "You know you are being perfectly absurd. You cannot make me believe you begrudge Phillip and Lucy the twins, when you have just spent a full hour making an absolute cake of yourself over them."

Francie rolled her eyes ceilingward at the newcomer's unannounced arrival. "That's all you know about it, Josephine Louise Powell," said Francie, coming about to regard the youngest of the Powell hopefuls with a jaundiced eye. "*You* do not have to live with Florence for two whole months. and I was *not* making a cake of myself."

"I'm afraid it appeared so to me, Francie," Josephine returned with a gentle smile of amusement. "You know you are dreadfully fond of little Emma and Evalina, not to mention young Patrick. You don't really wish Lucy had not been blessed with them."

"Pray don't be absurd, Jo," Francie retorted testily. "Of course I should never wish any such thing. It is only that the timing is so wretchedly inconvenient. Especially as Mama is determined to see me launched into Society this Season, when I should be perfectly willing to wait another year. If I did not know better, I should believe she is anxious to be rid of me."

"No, how can you even think such a thing?" Josephine demanded, her delicately wrought features expressive of disbelief mingled with troubled concern for her sister. "It is a shame things did not turn out quite the way you wanted. I know how much you were looking forward to having Lucy bring you out. On the other hand, does it not occur to you that the reason Mama has decided to remain at Greensward may not be so much because she is concerned about my health, but because she is worried about Florence's happiness?"

Francie, to whom such a possibility had not occurred, stared with a sudden, fixed expression at her younger sister. "No, why should it?" she asked warily of Josephine, who, possessed of a keen insight and a discerning nature which proved disconcertingly accurate more often than not, had the unhappy knack of arousing one's guilty conscience.

"Because you know Mama never does anything without a reason and because you have only to look at me to know that I am a deal stronger than I used to be. In case you had failed to notice, I am seldom ill these days, a fact that I overheard Mama mention to Papa not three weeks ago."

Francie, like her other siblings, had been used all her life to thinking of Josephine as sickly and, because of her sweet, unassuming nature, one to be fiercely protected. Naturally she had noticed that her little sister did indeed seem improved that winter. On the other hand, she was not so much better as to have lost her ethereal pallor. Neither, Francie noted with a small pang of regret, had she filled out sufficiently to be rid of her altogether too delicate appearance. Still, it would serve no one, and least of all Josephine, to point that out to her.

"But of course you are better, Jo," Francie said instead. "Still, I daresay Mama is right not to take you to London just when you *are* doing so well. Very likely she thinks you would do better here at home where you can take up your riding lessons again as soon as the weather permits. And you will admit the air is ever so much cleaner in the North Yorks than it could possibly be in the City."

"For pity's sake, Francie," Josephine snapped with a sudden, unwonted impatience. "I wish you will not treat me as if I were some silly creature without a brain in her head. I may not be robust like you, but I am neither an idiot nor a child. I am all of fourteen, old enough to know for myself that I should be better off in the country. On the other hand, I should do perfectly well at home without Mama in constant attendance. *I* am not the reason Mama has chosen to let Florence bring you out instead of performing that office herself. You would see that, if you would stop feeling sorry for yourself long enough to view things as they really are."

Francie, much taken aback at this uncharacteristic display of temper from the normally serene Josephine, could only acknowledge that her sister was right about one thing. She *had* been feeling sorry for herself. But then, faced with the prospect of having to dress up in ball gowns and behave in the manner of a proper young miss, only to be left cooling her heels on the sidelines among the other wallflowers, was reason enough to be less than enthused about the mean trick fate had played on her. At least with Lucy and Phillip, she could have been certain there would be some rollicking good adventures to make up for the less pleasurable aspects of a Season in London.

Lucy had promised to take her to see the riding school at Astley's Royal Amphitheatre and the new public billiards rooms at the Piazza at Covent Garden, among other curiosities—none of which Florence could possibly have countenanced. Not in her wildest imaginings could she picture Florence doing anything so daring as attending a session of Lady Wilhelmina Love's society of Epicureans, of which Lucy had become a member.

More significantly, however, Phillip was one of the Meltonian set, a bruising rider and a top of the trees Corinthian. In his company she had been sure to at least meet and perhaps even exchange a word or two with such famous horsemen as Lord Childe or, more importantly, the Earl of Ransome, Phillip's friend and comrade from the Peninsular campaign, who had once ridden in the face of French sharpshooters to bring aid to Phillip and his men. Phillip's tales of his friend's numerous heroic deeds had prompted her in one of her silly, childish moments, to swear that when she grew up, she would marry Ransome. Suffering a sharp stab of disappointment at the thought that she would not now in all likelihood so much as lay eyes on the fascinating nobleman, she became aware of how greatly she had looked forward to such a meeting. Indeed, she had counted most particularly on Phillip to bring the earl into her small sphere of influence. Ransome, after all, a noted rake and a gambler, made it a point to avoid the sort of *tonnish* parties to which she would be invited. Certainly, he would not be seen at Almack's Assembly Rooms. This fact, far from discrediting him in her eyes, served only to make him more attractive to Francie. Ransome, she doubted not, was a man after her own heart.

"Very well, Jo. You are neither a child nor an idiot. And I am perfectly aware that I have been indulging myself in self-pity. What has any of that to do with Florence's happiness? Florence and I have been at loggerheads for as long as I can remember. Far from contributing to her happiness, I shall be far more likely to disrupt her peace and tranquillity."

"Yes, you probably will," Jo agreed baldly. "On the other hand, perhaps what she needs is someone to give her a jolt. And just think, Francie, how much it must contribute to her feeling of self-confidence to realize Mama has chosen to entrust you into her care. Why, I daresay it will mean all the difference to Flo. If you cannot bring yourself to do it for Flo, then you might do it for yourself. After all, you have been itching to resolve the mystery surrounding Leighton's seeming disaffection. You know you have, Francie."

Francie, who could not deny the truth of that alle-

gation any more than she could dismiss the logic behind Josephine's explanation for their mama's motives, favored her younger sister with a moue of
disgust. "I shall thank you in future, Josephine Powell, never to disabuse me of my illusions. If you must
know, I am perfectly happy to remain in ignorance.
And pray do not think you will not pay for what you
have done. One of these days it will be your turn to
make your come-out in London and then, if there is
any justice in this world, you will be under *my* aegis."

Far from being intimidated by such a prospect,
Josephine appeared merely wistful. "It is doubtful
that I shall ever have a Season in London," she replied with simple candor. "But if that day should ever
come, Francie, you may be sure that I shall hold you
to your promise."

"Don't be a gaby, Jo," exclaimed Francie, who had
not paused to consider the possibility that Josephine's fragile constitution might indeed preclude
the rigors of a come-out in Society. It was, in fact, not
to be thought of. "You will have your fling in London."

"Do you think so, Francie?" murmured Jo, looking
suddenly very young and filled with doubts. "You are
not just saying that to make me feel better?"

"Stupid," said Francie, smiling as she hugged her
little sister about the shoulders. "Why should I wish
to make you feel better, when you have just coerced
me into doing something I shall most probably regret? The truth is that, though Flo has always been
the acknowledged Beauty of the family, you promise
fair, my dearest Jo, to put us all to the shade."

"Now, you are coming it much too strong. I know I shall never be a great beauty, but I should like to think I shall wear a beautiful gown one day and dance at my very own ball. I believe I should never ask for anything more if I could only have that."

"Then you are certain to have your wish come true, dearest Jo," Francie returned, leading Josephine into the secret passage that would take them to the duke's study, where they had left their papa in a vigorous debate with Lathrop over the authenticity of a manuscript alleged to have been authored by William Shakespeare and which the Earl of Bancroft had just purchased. "You will have your ball, I promise you."

Two

The day of Francie's departure for London dawned cold and dreary with mist. Hardly an auspicious beginning, she reflected, swallowing the lump in her throat as she waved good-bye to the gathering of Powells. Their numbers, minus the twins, Timothy and Thomas, who were away at school, and Florence, who awaited Francie's arrival in London, had begun to grow significantly smaller, she noted with a sudden pang. They had always seemed such a large and boisterous lot.

"Godspeed, my sweet," called her papa, the Earl of Bancroft, as the ancient, if well-preserved, family coach lurched into motion. "Do try and enjoy yourself. I daresay you will set London on its ear if you give it a chance."

"Indeed, dear. And pray remember," appended Lady Emmaline, "keep Daisy in attendance at all times. One never knows whom one might encounter in post inns."

"Yes, Mama. I shall," Francie shouted back, smiling through the mist of tears that clouded her vision. Then, as the coach entered the bend in the drive,

"Good-bye, Lucy," she called to her oldest sister and Phillip, who had come to speed her on her way. "Good-bye, Phillip. Good-bye, Jo."

Her last glimpse of the Powells was of her oldest brother, William Michael, who, lithely mounting one of his prime bloods, followed the coach for a few yards before waving and turning off, no doubt with the intent of seeing to the numerous tasks involved in the running of his father's estate.

Quelling a sigh, Francie settled back against the newly refurbished velvet squabs. Across from her, Daisy gave an audible groan and braced herself against the lurch and sway of the coach.

"Daisy, what is it?" exclaimed Francie solicitously. "Are you ill? You have gone white as a sheet."

"Beggin' your pardon, m'lady," said the abigail, the freckles standing out in sharp contrast to the pallor of her face, which had indeed assumed a hue somewhere between white and a sickly green. "I was fine until just a moment ago. Belike it's only that I ain't used to ridin'. I never been farther in my entire life than half a day's walk from Greensward."

"You poor dear. You are obviously prey to carriage sickness," Francie concluded, her heart sinking. "We shall turn back at once."

"Oh, no, m'lady. Not on my account, I beg you. I daresay I'll grow used to it before long, and then I'll be right as a trivet again, you'll see."

Francie gazed doubtfully at the maid servant, a girl little more than her own age. She had been recruited from the ranks of the downstairs maids to serve as Francie's abigail when it was discovered the girl had a certain natural flair for pressing and mending clothes and for arranging hair in neat, even modish, coiffures. "I fear, Daisy, it is not simply a matter of becoming used to the motion. Some people are just naturally poor travelers. You need not be embarrassed or ashamed. It is something that cannot be helped. I really think you would do better to stay home. No doubt we can find someone else to stand in for you."

"Oh, no, m'lady, I beg you," wailed Daisy with a look of mortification. "My ma was that proud of me for being picked to serve as your lady's maid. I wouldn't want to disappoint her all on account of me being such a poor creature. And, besides, I might never have another chance to see what lies beyond the moors. I'll be all right, I promise you. Only, please don't leave me at home, m'lady."

Francie visibly wavered before that earnest plea. Though she herself had rebelled at the idea of being shipped off to London like a package of goods to be put on display for the highest bidder, she understood Daisy's yearning to see something of the world. After all, Francie had always had a keen spirit of adventure and, under different circumstances, would have been excited at the prospect of such a journey as this promised to be. It was only that she doubted not that her sister Flo would succeed in taking all the flair out of a visit to London. It was hardly in Flo's nature to do otherwise.

"Very well, Daisy," Francie conceded against her better judgment. "I shan't insist on returning. But

do give fair warning if you feel yourself on the verge
of needing to pull over."

"Yes, m'lady," agreed the abigail, assaying a wan
smile as the coach left the drive and entered the track
that would take them to the road to Malton and from
there to York and beyond.

Francie settled back against the squabs with a sigh
and gazed out the window at the passing landscape of
rolling downs and heather-covered moors. A pity her
papa could not be persuaded to let her ride Jester
behind the coach. She would soon be bored to tears
being cooped up with Daisy in the swaying confines
of the old conveyance with nothing better to do than
twiddle her thumbs. It really was not in the least fair.
Were she a boy, she might have driven her own curricle and pair to London. Thanks to Phillip's tutor-
ing, she could drive at a splitting pace and feather-edge
a blind corner better than most men she knew. Phillip, who was indisputably a top-sawyer himself, said
she had been blessed with a natural gift for driving.

The morning passed as it had begun, with the mist
altering to a steady drizzle that did not let up the rest
of the day. Pausing only long enough to breathe the
horses at regular intervals, they made excellent time.
Still, Francie, who had partaken of a basket lunch in
the coach and who consequently had had little opportunity to stretch her legs, could only be glad when
at last as night overtook them they reached the post-
ing inn and the rooms her father had sent ahead to
reserve for her.

The inn on the outskirts of Crowle, while picturesquely rustic, offered little in the way of interest,

Francie decided, taking in at a glance the half-timbered two-story house covered in clematis and ivy. Save for a curricle and a showy pair of high-steppers in the care of a young tiger, who by all rights should have been long since in his bed, the inn yard was all but deserted.

"Here we be, m'lady," said John Wiggens, the coachman, opening the door and helping his mistress to alight. "Toby, here, will see you in while I look to the cattle," he added, indicating the footman in green and yellow livery who had been assigned to accompany the coach to London. Encumbered with the travel cases and bandboxes the two women would require for the night, Toby stood respectfully at attention.

"Thank you, Wiggens," smiled Francie, turning to lend Daisy a steadying hand. "Have the coach ready at dawn, if you please. We shall want an early start if we are to make Melton Mowbray before dusk."

The groom noticeably hesitated at this pronouncement from his mistress. "Er—beggin' your pardon, Lady Francie," he ventured, turning his hat in his hands, "but about Melton Mowbray."

Wiggens, a retainer of long standing who had put Francie on her first horse, nervously shifted his weight, Francie noted with a sudden sense of foreboding. Now what the devil, she wondered, steeling herself for bad news. "Yes, Wiggens? What about Melton Mowbray?"

The man coughed to clear his throat. "Lady Francie, it be out of our way, as you well know. An', well, the word here is that 'tis the gatherin' of the Quorn.

The town is sure to be crowded with all manner of gentlemen. Belike we'd do better to stay on the London Road and avoid what might prove an unpleasantness."

If he had hoped by this to deter her from her chosen course, he was soon proved well short of the mark. His young mistress's face positively beamed at the prospect. "The gathering of the Quorn, Wiggens?" she exclaimed in obvious alt. "But how simply marvelous. Indeed, I never hoped for such luck when I persuaded Papa to allow me this one request. To see the Quorn country was one thing, but the hunt itself. Why, I should not miss it for the world."

"Yes, m'lady," agreed the coachman with a noticeable lack of enthusiasm. Having spent his entire life in the service of the gentry, he had few illusions as to the dire possibilities inherent in introducing a lovely innocent like Lady Francine into the midst of a throng of Meltonians gathered for a meet. It would be, he reflected dourly as he turned to the task of bedding the cattle, like dropping a vixen into the middle of a pack of hungry hounds. Only, knowing his spirited young mistress the way he did, he doubted not it would be the hounds who would soon find themselves routed rather than the vixen.

"Did you hear, Daisy?" Francie was saying as she led the dazed abigail into the inn. "It is the gathering of the Quorn at Melton Mowbray." In her excitement, she hardly noted Toby, who, saying he would just go and fetch the innkeeper, left the two women standing in the common room. "Oh, what I should not give to be a boy and ride in that greatest of all hunts. To think

Flying William Childe himself set the standard for all
the others, there, in the Quorn country. Hugo Meynell, the Master of the Quorn, will be there, and I
daresay the Earl of Ransome will put in an appearance.
There could hardly be a meeting of the Quorn without
him. Phillip says Ransome is the finest horseman ever
to ride to hounds. How I should like to see him in 'the
quick thing.' Only the most daring huntsmen ride in
that mad dash to stay with the hounds across fields
and fences. I daresay a double oxer fence would be
an obstacle of little significance to someone with the
cold nerve of a man like Ransome."

"Ranshome? Beg your pardon, little lady," spoke
up a slurred masculine voice at Francie's elbow, "but
if it'sh Earl of Ransome you mean, you've queer notion of hish lordship. Why, he hashn't any nerves at
all, or anything, for that matter, to recommend him
to th' likesh of you. Expect your mama and papa
would take exception if they heard you puffing off
the consequence of man like him. Case you didn't
know it, Ranshome's noted rakeshame and gambler.
Hardly the sort for pretty little mish like you to be
moonin' over."

Francie's first instinct at being accosted by a
stranger, to remove herself without disdaining so
much as a word, went into sudden eclipse at this un-
warranted attack on a man who had the distinction
of being not only her brother-in-law's friend, but a
war hero of no little note. That he was also a gambler
and a rake was of little significance, after all, when
one took into account his other, far more important
attributes. He had saved Phillip's life at grave risk to

his own, and he was a bruising rider to the hounds. Whatever else he might be, he did not deserve to have his name sullied by strangers.

"I beg your pardon," exclaimed Francie, turning to regard with chilly disfavor a middle-aged gentleman, whose flashy dress, replete with ruffles and lace, proclaimed one who aspired to dandyism, while his flushed face and disheveled appearance gave mute evidence of one well to live. "As it happens, I am well acquainted with the earl's reputation, which is why I fear it is you who are mistaken. I know for a fact that his lordship is a man of rare courage and honor, and if I were a man, I should make you think better of making aspersions against his character."

"The devil you would," the would-be dandy returned, his aspect noticeably changing. Francie's cheeks flushed and her chin rose a fraction of an inch as Sir Fancy-Lace, an obvious bounder, deliberately ran his eyes over her from her straw carriage hat with the blue ribbons to match her traveling dress to her dainty feet clad in blue kid half-boots, then back again. "Intimately acquainted with Ranshome, are you?"

Behind Francie, Daisy gave a nervous cough, and Francie, suddenly reminded of her mama's dire warning not to talk to strangers, was made belatedly aware of the wisdom of such advice. She only just managed to suppress a sigh of relief at the sight of Toby, coming toward them in the company of the innkeeper, a reassuringly stout-looking individual with an apron tied around his middle.

"Whether I am or not is hardly any of your affair,"

she retorted in withering accents. Far from being of the Meltonian set, the stranger was clearly on the order of a country squire with grandiose notions. "Suffice it to say that his lordship would look with disfavor on any man who so far forgot himself as to behave in a rude fashion toward a lady. And now you will no doubt pardon me. I have better things to do than stand around and exchange words with a gentleman of questionable manners to whom I have not been properly introduced. Come, Daisy," she added, shoving loftily past the gaping stranger.

Too late. An uncouth hand clamped hard about her arm and held her.

"Little shpitfire, ain't you," growled the dandified country squire. "You've a sharp tongue for a female, traveling without the benefit of a man to protect her." The oaf's expression, Francie noted with rising color, had turned distinctly ugly. "Maybe you ain't the lady I took you for."

Francie's lovely eyes flashed blue sparks of outrage. How dared the lout lay a hand on her! Worse, however, was the lowering certainty that he took her for one of Ransome's ladybirds. The cad! she fumed, and then was made instantly aware that a soft thrill coursed down the length of her even at so absurd a notion. She, after all, was hardly the sort with whom a man like Ransome would choose to set up so much as a light flirtation. Far from minding such a thought, it occurred to her that very likely being the object of Ransome's amorous attentions might very well be the most delectable sort of adventure. Certainly, she would rather be sunk beneath reproach than stoop to pointing out to Sir Fancy-Lace that, far from traveling unaccompanied, she was attended by both a footman and a lady's maid.

"And you, sir," she said, disdainfully snatching her arm from his grasp, "are clearly no gentleman." Noting the angry leap of the man's eyes, followed by a look of cunning, Francie was reminded of her sister Lucy's latest novella about the dark Lord of Bartleby Castle who broke down the door with the intent of ravishing the fair Lady Hortensia in an inn very much on the order of this one. The next words were out of her mouth before she thought. "You may be certain Ransome shall hear of this on the morrow, when I pay my respects to him at Melton Mowbray. The earl is a dear friend of my brother-in-law, who just happens to be the Duke of Lathrop. I am, furthermore, on my way to Melton Mowbray for the express purpose of meeting the Earl of Ransome. I am, you see, sworn to marry his lordship."

Francie had the immediate satisfaction of beholding the squire's face go a sudden sickly shade of grey just before she turned on her heel and made her exit in the grand manner with Daisy, looking little better than the squire, following hastily after her.

"Faith, m'lady," whispered the scandalized abigail as soon as they were safely out of the common room, "what have you gone and done?"

"Why, nothing, Daisy," Francie returned, assaying a cool composure that was in sharp contrast to the rapid beating of her heart, "save only to tell a little white lie in order to discourage Sir Fancy-Lace from making a further nuisance of himself. So unmannerly

a brute might not think twice about breaking in on
a nobody without the benefit of a man to protect her,
but you may be sure the promised bride of the Earl
of Ransome is a different proposition altogether. I
believe we shall not be bothered again by the besotted squire."

" 'Tis a lie, for certain, Lady Francie," commented
the abigail, her face expressive of doubt, "but as to
the size of it, I fear it may in the end prove bigger
than Lady Lucy's fish stories, not to mention her tales
of a romantical nature. If his lordship, the Earl of
Ransome, should hear he has a bride in the offing,
I fear he might not think it a laughing matter."

Francie was, somewhat belatedly, having misgivings
of a similar nature. She experienced a queasy sensation at this all too accurate assessment of the dire
consequences of what she had done. Still, a man like
Ransome, who was noted for his valor and cunning
in battle, would hardly hold it against her for employ-
ing such a ruse. She doubted not that, if the worst
should happen, his lordship would not only understand that she had been merely taking a precaution-
ary step to protect herself, but would appreciate the
resourcefulness that had prompted it. And if he did
not, it was far too late to change things now, she reflected practically. She had been in hot water far too
many times in her short life not to have learned that
there was little point in borrowing trouble. She
sighed fatalistically. Whatever came of her brashness
would come, and no amount of worrying over it
would make the slightest difference, one way or the
other. Indeed, the most she could do at this stage was

to remind herself of her mama's oft-repeated advice to curb her impulsiveness and in future think things through before she acted.

Having thus thought this particular matter through, if somewhat after the fact, Francie shrugged away any lingering doubts. "Nonsense, Daisy. I daresay there is not the least chance the earl will ever hear of it. After all, Sir Fancy-Lace is hardly the sort to rub elbows with members of the Meltonian set. Now, let us speak no more of it. We are both tired and hungry. I see no reason to spoil the evening with pointless speculations."

After a night's rest, undisturbed either by troubling qualms or by rude, drunken squires, Francine rose refreshed and eager to set out on the second leg of the journey, which would bring her into the open grazing grounds of the Quorn country. Indeed, she could not but be aware that she fairly tingled with excitement at the prospect. With any luck, they might even arrive in time to come upon the hunt itself. The only thing she could think of that would equal such a thrill was to be able to put Jester through his paces if only for a short ride across the wolds. And, indeed, why should she not? she mused, her blood quickening at the very prospect of being able to say, if only to herself, that she had actually ridden in the Quorn country.

Oh, it was simply too delectable an adventure to miss! It might, in fact, be her *only* adventure in what promised to be an otherwise tedious two months away from home. And, after all, what was the worst that could happen? She was unknown outside the immediate vicinity of Greensward, a condition that was unlikely to be altered by her come-out in London. She, after all, was hardly the sort to cut a dash in Society. She need only make certain to be back in the coach long before her little cortege actually reached the Pork Pie Inn on the outskirts of Melton Mowbray. She doubted not that, other than Daisy, Wiggens, and Toby, no one would ever be the wiser.

Daisy, noting some little time later the militant sparkle in her mistress's eye, judiciously kept her tongue between her teeth as she helped Francie don the new riding habit of Nile blue with pantaloons beneath the skirt, and boots. Nor did she venture a word, much as she might wish to have done, when Francie eschewed the straw carriage hat for the smart beaver, which, besides boasting a low crown and narrow brim, sported an ostrich plume dyed to match her dress.

Lady Francine, Daisy knew, was up to something, which was hardly surprising. Of the earl's four daughters, Lady Francine was ever the one to be off trying some new, hair-raising stunt, which had given her mama not a few anxious moments. Daisy herself had overheard Lady Emmaline say once that, while she had always wished her children to face life bravely, she preferred Francine might do so with a mite less of death-defying exuberance. The daredevil of the earl's brood had ever been on the brink of disaster, reflected the abigail, suppressing a sigh of foreboding, as, some moments later, she followed her mistress out to the waiting coach.

Wiggens, likewise, was given to reflect on the dire unpredictability of his young mistress when he laid eyes on her in riding clothes. Nor was he made any easier when, contrary to his first expectations, she calmly allowed herself to be handed up into the coach as if it were perfectly natural to undertake a drive decked out in a riding habit and boots. Indeed, nothing short of her ordering him to stay to the London Road in lieu of visiting Melton Mowbray would have relieved him of the dread suspicion that the cunning little minx meant to take to horseback as soon as ever they entered the Quorn country.

Briefly he considered leaving her saddle and bridle at the inn to be retrieved on the return trip, only to discard the notion almost as soon as it was conceived. Lady Francie was perfectly capable of determining to ride bareback and astride with naught but a rope hackamore for a bridle did she truly have her heart set on putting Jester through his paces across that most famous of hunting grounds. It would be bad enough having to inform the earl that his daughter had disgraced herself by insinuating herself into the meeting of the Quorn without further having to confess that she had done so in a manner wholly unbefitting a female of refinement. At last reflecting with a sigh that he was at any rate nigh the age of retirement and that perhaps it might not be wholly intolerable to remove a trifle earlier than planned to his daughter's cottage outside of Whitby, Bancroft's long-time retainer climbed to the driving box and set the restive team in motion.

The Quorn country, undulating grassy wolds, was everything that Francie had imagined it to be, and more. How different from her beloved moors and downs were the maze of narrow lanes, half-hidden by high hedges and tall trees, the green, rolling sheep pastures interrupted without warning by cool spinneys, and the sudden cottages of pale pink stone with their neat roofs either of thatch or slate. Had she not insisted on abandoning the coach some time past for the freedom of traveling by horseback, her view of the open fields would have been severely restricted, she reflected, and grinned at the memory of Wiggens's useless arguments against putting her up on Jester.

For the past hour, she had held Jester to a smooth, easy gait, which kept her in sight of the coach and yet allowed her to rejoice in the feeling of having a horse once more beneath her. If only she had not to keep to a sedate pace, she reflected, gazing with yearning eyes out over the wolds. She doubted not she would have to return to the coach before very much longer, and the thought of its cramped quarters held little appeal after her invigorating ride on Jester.

Hardly had that thought crossed her mind when suddenly she straightened to what sounded very like the distant blare of a trumpet. "Faith, Jester, did you hear that?" she exclaimed, pulling the stallion to a halt. Her ears strained to catch the faint, but unmistakable, baying of hounds on the scent. "It's the hunt, Jester. And I daresay they are coming in this direction. Oh, if only I had not the hedge in the way."

Forgetting everything but her eagerness to catch an unimpeded glimpse of the chase, she lifted Jester into a canter along the hedge in search of a break in the foliage. The blare of the trumpet and the baying of the pack crescendoed behind and to her right as the field of huntsmen spilled over a hill in a frenetic swell of hounds and horses. Francie, spotting a low place in the hedge, sent Jester at it, reaching across the road at an angle.

Leaning forward in the saddle, Francie flung her heart over before her. She clung, thrilling to the stallion's smooth, powerful flight, as Jester soared up and over the hedge.

The stallion lit, running, Francie, riding easily in the saddle. Less than a hundred yards away raced the pack, stretched out over the field with the huntsmen strung out behind and two hounds far in the lead.

At the lead hounds's heels, mounted on a great brute of a horse with a large, ugly head and powerful neck, a rangy body to match the long legs and great muscled hind quarters, a single horseman rode. Francie had never seen such a horse or such a rider before. Fearless, a vision of controlled power and reckless daring, horse and rider took fences, hillocks, and the occasional, unexpected ditch with hardly a break in stride. They were utterly magnificent together.

With eyes only for the two hounds and that single rider, Francie caught little more than a glimpse of the

fox as it whisked over a double oxer and disappeared
from view. With bated breath, Francie watched the
lead hounds, tongues hanging, bound in a straight
line after it. In an instant they were over the railed
hedge, and, behind them, the bay horse was gathering
for the leap.

The exultant cry swelled from her throat—"Tal-
lyho!"—as the marvelous creature sailed in a flying
leap over the obstacle.

Later, she was to suppose she had been quite out
of her head with excitement. Certainly, her blood
surged in her veins, and she was in the grips of what
her mama was wont to call an overpowering passion—something to which, Lady Emmaline did not
scruple to note, her third daughter was inordinately
prone. And in truth, Francie doubted that anyone,
save perhaps her prim and proper sister Florence,
could have resisted so mad or glorious an impulse.
Whatever the case, one moment she was holding
Jester down to a canter, and the very next she was
leaning forward in the saddle, calling to the very best
in the stallion.

Her heart swelled with pride as she felt Jester's
great surge to the fore. Then the fence was before
them, looming suddenly large and exceedingly formidable with its broad hedge embraced on either
side by rails. The pack of hounds swarmed past the
racing stallion in a frenzied dash to catch the leaders.
It was wonderful, glorious. Carried on a swell of excitement, Francie sent Jester straight for the barrier.

* * *

Henry Marcus Danvers, the Earl of Ransome, better known to his closest intimates as Harry, pulled
the iron-jawed Brutus to a stamping halt. Before him,
the pair of hounds whined and trotted back and
forth, their noses to the ground as they cast about
for the lost scent.

The fox had gone underground and very likely,
having made its escape by way of a back door, was
even then putting a goodly distance between itself
and its trackers. It was just as well, thought Ransome,
glancing over his shoulder in search of the outdis-
tanced pack of hounds and riders. It was only an hour
to dusk, and as far as he was concerned the hunt had
already served its purpose. The feeling of ennui with
which he had been plagued for longer than he cared
to admit had been momentarily dispelled by a crack
dash over the Quorn country.

It was his sole purpose in coming to the meet, he
realized with a sardonic twist of handsome lips—for
the chase and not the kill.

He must be getting old, he mused; and, indeed, at
nine and twenty, he was uncommonly weary of those
pursuits that he had once considered not only vastly
entertaining, but of profound importance in his life
as well. But then, nothing had seemed the same since
he had given up his commission and returned home
from the Continent. He supposed he would have
been surprised had it been otherwise. At least on the
Continent, between foraging for food behind enemy
lines and eluding capture by the French, not to mention skirmishing with Spanish bandits and French soldiers, there had been little time for boredom, he

reflected. He was cynically amused at his disaffection with the even tenor of his life since his father had been so disobliging as to succumb to a fatal inflammation of the lungs over a twelvemonth past, leaving Harry the title. Not even Harry's gaming house, the Goldfinch, quixotically named after an exotic Portuguese singer with whom Harry had enjoyed a brief, if colorful, alliance, had served to completely eradicate the feeling that his existence had begun to pall on him. But then, the test of nerve involved in laying a wager on the turn of a card was only a pale facsimile of what a soldier experienced in war. The various games of chance in which he indulged himself, after all, entailed only the risk of a little blunt. On the Continent there had been a great deal more at stake, not the least of which was the welfare of England.

Suddenly he laughed, grimly amused at the direction in which his reveries had taken him. Bloody hell, he was bored indeed if he had come to think of returning to the cursed fighting as something even remotely desirable.

It was at that point that the blare of the trumpet and the swarming of the pack over the double oxer brought him back to the present. Halted on the brow of a low hill, he had a clear view of the hunt's progress. Hugo Meynell, the Master of the Quorn, mounted on his big grey, stood out among perhaps half a dozen riders hard on the heels of the pack's stragglers. Behind them, the rest of the hunt trailed in small bunches or were strung out in singles and pairs.

Instantly Ransome's gaze narrowed on a flash of blue atop a long-legged chestnut alone in the midst of the pack of hounds. Now, what the devil? he wondered. Even had the dash of color not stood out amid the sea of Meltonian black, he would have picked the slim rider out at once as an interloper. The sleek thoroughbred would have taken his eye, if nothing else. Ransome was familiar with every prime bit of blood in the meet, and this was one to inspire feelings of covetousness. More than that, however, the fool rode with a fearlessness that compelled if not admiration, then a wry appreciation of what appeared to be an utter disregard of self. He watched with detached interest as the lone rider sent the chestnut unhesitatingly at the railed hedge.

Any double oxer was a jump to test the mettle of hunter and huntsman, but this one, Ransome reflected, recalling his own recent hurtle over the barrier, had the added hazard of a standing pool of water on the blind side, a remnant of the previous evening's shower, no doubt. If either the horse or the rider entertained second thoughts at the crucial moment, one or both were in for a nasty spill.

Suddenly Ransome stiffened, as it came to him what was most peculiar about the young daredevil.

"Good God," he breathed. "A woman!"

His previous detachment dissipated in that stupendous moment of realization. He sat, frozen in dire expectation of being made witness to what must inevitably prove a tragedy. Still, the female, whoever she was, could ride, by God. Reluctant admiration was wrung from him as he watched her lean forward in the saddle, heard her call to the stallion. His hand clenched on the reins as the chestnut left the ground in a powerful leap. He neither moved nor breathed as horse and rider appeared to hang in the air. Then the chestnut struck the pool, sending silvery sheets of water cascading upwards about the magnificent chest and shoulders. The stallion lunged out, sure of foot, onto dry ground, and the girl, with a wild peal of what must clearly have been exultation, began at once to pull the animal in.

Sidling beneath the firm hand on the reins, the stallion came to a stop.

"Jester, you beauty, you," exclaimed the girl, running a hand over the arched neck, darkened with sweat. "You did it. I knew you would. There never was a more wonderful horse than you."

It was only then, as she straightened, that she became aware of Ransome seated on the rangy bay, watching her from the hilltop, while, behind her, horses and riders surged or scrambled over the double oxer.

With perhaps a hundred yards between them, Ransome could tell little about her, save that she was young, slender, and presented a breathtaking vision of spirited femininity atop the tall chestnut. A slow smile of appreciation curved his lips, as, deliberately, he lifted his quirt to the brim of his hat in silent tribute.

He sensed the girl's blush as, ducking her head, she brought her wheeling mount back to the fore. Then acknowledging Ransome's salute with a wholly impetuous toss of her regal head, she sent the stallion at a lope for the road to Melton Mowbray.

"Oh, yes, my young beauty. At least you have *some*

notions of self-preservation," murmured Ransome,
watching that fleeting figure jump the hedge cleanly
into the road, where a coach appeared to be waiting
for her. "You will do far better to keep your identity
a secret. A pity we could not become better acquainted. I have a feeling we might have come to enjoy
one another's company."

With a faint, sardonic smile, he saw the trim figure
slip lightly from the saddle, then turn for a last, fleeting glance at him before she disappeared into the
confines of the coach.

The next moment, he was surrounded by plunging
horses and riders.

"Someone we know?" queried Edward Rutledge,
Viscount Laverly, his glance following Ransome's.

Ransome replied absently without taking his gaze
off the departing coach. "I shouldn't think so."

"A kindred spirit, no doubt," speculated Laverly.

"At the very least, a complete and utter hoyden."
Ransome quelled an absurd prickle at the nape of
his neck. "Curious."

Laverly elevated a quizzically amused eyebrow.
"What is that, old man?"

Ransome looked at him and shrugged. "The
strangest feeling that I have just been jabbed between
the shoulder blades by a quixotic finger of fate. No
doubt it is only a lingering effect of the beef and
kidneys with which I indulged myself at breakfast."

Three

The inn's cobblestoned yard, embraced on three sides by a three-story edifice with balconies and boasting a great, spreading oak tree in one corner, was bustling with activity as Francie, stepping down from the coach, turned to lend Daisy a supporting hand. A flurry of hostlers were hurriedly leading a fresh team into the traces of a post chaise while others catered to the needs of the huntsmen who were putting up at the inn with their strings of hunters. Francie firmly led the reeling abigail through the melee of men and horses.

"Belike Mr. Wiggens was right, m'lady, and we ought t've gone on to Oakham," suggested Daisy, who, in spite of her obvious relief at finding herself at last on solid ground, was moved to make an effort to save her mistress from what she perceived to be a potential quagmire of mischance. "There's a powerful lot of gentlemen at the inn."

Francie, still prey to a mixture of emotions in the wake of having succumbed to irresistible impulse, not the least of which was the uneasy suspicion that she might have miscalculated the possible repercussions of her mad dash across the wold, smiled absently and shook her head.

"Nonsense, Daisy. You know you could not bear another mile, let alone fifteen, in the coach."

Even as she went on to assure the abigail that they would do well enough tucked away in their rooms, her glance moved ceaselessly over the sea of faces around her in search of one that, in spite of the fact that she had been too far away to see it with any real clarity, she was quite certain she would recognize immediately.

Blast the luck! she thought with a wry quirk of the lips. The hounds *would* have to lose the scent within sight of her own plunge into what Flo called her younger sister's predilection for iniquitous behavior. And yet how glorious it had been to ride neck or nothing across even so small a stretch of the Quorn country! She could not regret it no matter what might come of it any more than she could regret the madness that had compelled her to put her fate to the touch on that wonderful, wholly magnificent final jump.

If only *he* had not been there to witness it, she reflected, and was made immediately aware by a soft, rebellious thrill through her midriff that some small part of her was not in the least sorry that he, of all people, had seen her in her moment of triumph. And how not? she mused with an irrepressible grin. After all, an adventure, especially an adventure of magnificent proportions such as this one, was made all the more delectable when it was shared with someone, even if, as in this case, the sharing was wholly inadvertent and fraught with the possibility of dire consequences.

What a strange panoply of feelings had washed over her upon looking up to discover she had not escaped without notice! A flush suffused her from head to toe at the memory of that tall, compelling figure, watching her from the back of the powerful bay.

The sudden queasy sensation in the pit of her stomach had hardly been an unfamiliar one, she mused. She had experienced it far too many times in her life to mistake it for what it was—the natural reaction to having been caught in the act of transgressing the bounds of what was considered proper for one of her gender. Dash it all, she thought. Little as she enjoyed the unpleasant aftermaths of her frequent excursions into dangerous waters, it seemed she was forever doomed to plunge headlong into them. But then, she did not see how she could resist being true to her nature. One might as well demand that she willingly cease to breathe, she told herself, quelling the small echo of her dearest papa's admonitions that one was given the gift of reason for the very purpose of thinking before leaping. It was all very well in theory to go through life governed by the purely rational, but Francie could not but believe such an existence would be just a trifle flat. She, after all, was no stranger to the flush of excitement that had pervaded her entire body that afternoon, the intoxicating feeling of breathlessness, the heady rush of blood through her veins. These, like the sheer joy of racing with fearless abandon on a swift horse, she had

known many times before, but never in the context
of finding herself under the scrutiny of a gentleman.

Her immediate, subsequent reaction had, perhaps
understandably, been one of confusion, which had
only been intensified by the gentleman's deliberate
and, she doubted not, odiously mocking salute. Francie was forced to stifle a groan at the memory. What
a fool she had been to think she could pull off such
a stunt with impunity. And yet, true to the streak of
perversity that no amount of her mama's gentle curtain lectures or discomfitingly penetrating looks of
understanding could eradicate, she had given in to
the impulse to acknowledge him with what undoubtedly had appeared an unforgivable brazenness.

The devil, she thought, wondering, not for the first
time, who and what manner of gentleman he was.
Recalling that assured ease in the saddle that had so
much characterized him, as had the commanding
cast of the magnificently broad shoulders and powerfully knit frame, not to mention the impression of
careless humor that had seemed to emanate from
him, she thought that under different circumstances
she would have liked him very well. He had seemed
to embrace the dauntlessness of spirit that appealed
to her own unruly streak of adventurousness. Whatever she might or might not have felt for him, however, was now clearly beside the point.

She had ruined herself before ever having set foot
in London, and, while she did not mind it so much
for herself, she could not but feel a twinge of guilt
when she thought of the probable reaction to the

news of the host of Powells who had entertained such
high expectations for her.

Still, she reflected wryly, there was nothing for it
now but to forge ahead. To do less would be to show
craven, and she would rather die than have it be said
Francine Elizabeth Powell had flinched in the face
of adversity. If she had sunk herself beneath reproach, what could it possibly matter anyway? she
thought rebelliously. She had never entertained any
illusions that she would be a success in the fashionable world. She would leave all that for her brothers
and sisters. She, after all, would be perfectly content
to remain in the country, unfettered by convention.

"There now, Daisy," Francie crooned some minutes later, as she helped the abigail to a cot set out
for the servant in the dressing room. "You just lie
down and rest for a while. I daresay you will be feeling
more the thing after a night's sleep."

"But I shouldn't, m'lady," Daisy feebly protested.
"I hadn't ought to leave you to look after yourself."

"I have been looking after myself for almost as long
as I can remember. You may be sure I am perfectly
capable of doing so for another night. Are you quite
certain you will have nothing to eat?"

"Indeed, no, m'lady," Daisy replied with a grimace.
"I'm afraid I could not even look at a bite."

"Well, perhaps in the morning, then," Francie conceded. "You just go to sleep. I promise I shall awaken
you if I feel the least need for your services."

Hardly had Francie spread the counterpane over
her reluctant abigail and softly closed the door to the
dressing room behind her, however, than she was suf-

fused with a restlessness that not even the hearty mutton stew the innkeeper had sent up to her could assuage. Not in the least inclined for bed, she soon found the cozy confines of her room unbearably stifling. Nor did it help that the unmistakably festive rumble and occasional roar of masculine voices carried to her quite clearly from the common room belowstairs. Indeed, she thought whimsically, the very air seemed to crackle with electricity generated by the gathering of males in primal celebration of the hunt.

How very unfair and yet typical of her fate that she should be relegated to lonely solitude in her room merely because of an accident of birth, Francie mused wryly. If she were a boy, she might at least have been allowed the freedom to frequent the common room. If only she could take a stroll in the night air, she thought longingly, sure that that would be sufficient to quiet her overstimulated nerves.

Recognizing the voice of temptation, she caught herself immediately. It was one thing to give in to irresistible impulse, but quite another to deliberately court disaster. Still, there could hardly be any objection to her stepping out on the terrace under the cover of night just for a moment or two, she reasoned, finding herself at the window that opened up onto that quaint feature of the Pork Pie Inn.

The next instant, she had slipped her pelisse on over the walking dress into which she had taken the precaution of changing on the outskirts of the town. Releasing the window latch, she pushed open the sashes and stepped out onto the terrace.

With the arrival of the supper hour, the courtyard had settled into a peaceful quiet disturbed only by the drone of voices, punctuated by an occasional outburst of laughter, that issued from the inn itself. Content to drink in the brisk night air, Francie made no attempt to make heads or tails of the tendrils of conversation wafting her way as she strolled along the terrace.

She was, consequently, taken unawares by the sudden, distinct impingement of a familiar name on her consciousness.

"The bloody Marquis of Leighton again. Hell and the devil confound him and his meddling," grated a harsh voice marked by unmistakable rancor. "Something will have to be done about him, and soon, or not even your precious Madame Noire will be enough to keep him satisfied. You and I are like to find ourselves swinging from the bloody gallows."

"Calm yourself, old man," cautioned a second voice, made distinctive by a soft, drawling arrogance of tone. Inexplicably, Francie felt a chill course down her spine at its utter lack of passion. "You exaggerate, surely. It is true Leighton has made himself something of a nuisance, but I hardly think things are so desperate as you imagine."

Francie, tingling with a thrilling sense of danger, peered cautiously over the balustrade down into the shadow-draped courtyard. The red glow of a cheroot drew her attention to the darker shadows of two men standing in close conversation nearly directly beneath her. She could discern nothing of their features in the gloom and little of their forms, save that one, somewhat taller than the other and slenderly built, presented a languorous aspect all the more sinister, somehow, for its very appearance of lazy indifference. Of the two, Francie immediately sensed he was the more dangerous.

"Then you are a fool," pronounced the shorter of the two. "Leighton, in case you have forgotten, has a young bride at home. A beauty, too, if all I hear is true. It seems a mite queer to me that a man who has never been known to be in the petticoat line would suddenly fall head over ears for a bloody actress. It has a rotten stench to it, I tell you."

The cheroot's red glow sketched an arc through the air, then shattered in a burst of sparks against the cobblestones. "What you say may be true," came back in slow, languorous accents. "Perhaps you are unaware of the rumors, however. It seems the new marchioness may be somewhat lacking in the warmer instincts."

Francie clenched her fists in outrage at so unfair an aspersion against her sister. Flo might be a stickler for the proprieties, but she was hardly a cold fish. She was a Powell, after all, and, if there was one thing the Powells had never lacked, it was the propensity for passionate natures.

"The devil, you say," came the reply in grating amusement. "The marquis got himself an ice queen, did he?"

An indolent shoulder lifted in a shrug. "He would not be the first man to be taken in by a pretty face. More importantly, you may be sure La Belle Noire will know precisely how to use it to our advantage.

She is a woman of many talents, as Leighton will discover should he become more than a mere nuisance. Even a marquis is not immune to a thrust of hard steel in the back."

Francie's cheeks paled with horror at the second villain's answer, a coarse bark of laughter. Indeed, she was forced to clap a hand to her mouth in order to stifle a gasp. Still, she must have made some sound, or a betraying movement, perhaps.

Her blood chilled at a sudden "h-s-s-s-t!" from below. Hastily, she stepped back into the shadows, her heart thumping madly.

"Bloody hell. I heard something. Up there, on the balcony."

"The breeze, no doubt, playing among the vines," came in speculative accents.

Silence fell, broken only by the plaintive hoot of an owl and the drone of voices from inside the inn. Francie held her breath and waited.

The seconds ticked by with painful slowness, until Francie began to hope that the two men had simply stolen away. Carefully, she drew in a long, shuddering breath and eased away from the wall. Thinking that the cozy room she had left was far preferable to being caught out on the terrace by a pair of murderous villains, she turned to go back the way she had come, only to freeze in her tracks.

The furtive shadow at the far end of the terrace seemed to leap out of the gloom, a menacing presence; and, behind her, came the distinct scrape of shoe leather against the wooden steps leading up to the terrace from the courtyard. The devil, she thought. She had allowed herself to be trapped as neatly as a rabbit in a snare.

That less than heartening realization might have sent a less enterprising female into a sudden gloom. Francie, however, was cast of a different mold. Hardly had she come to a chilling assessment of her predicament than her glance lit on the sprawling shape of the ancient oak with its magnificent spread of branches reaching almost to the terrace itself. A grin flashed across her face. The next instant, she was across the terrace and poised on top of the balustrade rail. Flinging her heart before her, she leaped.

She wished her brothers Timothy and Tom could be there to see her as, landing with the agility born of years of practice, she stepped noiselessly along a massive arm of the tree to the trunk. From there it would be child's play to slip from one branch to the next until she could safely drop to the ground.

She might have wished for her father and her older brother Will's presence as well, she decided, as it was soon brought home to her that she was not out of the briars yet.

"Hellsfire! There was someone here, I tell you," carried distinctly to her ears.

"I never doubted you for a moment. The culprit has undoubtedly given us the slip. Indeed, if I am not mistaken, he is even now making his way down that tree."

"The devil he is!"

As that outburst was accompanied by the distinct rap of bootsoles heading in the direction of the outside stairs to the terrace, Francie hastily abandoned any pretense of hiding. Dropping to the ground, she picked up her skirts and ran for the inn.

Later it was to occur to her that perhaps she would have done better to flee to John Wiggens in the stables. Certainly, she had the distinct feeling of having leaped from the frying pan into the fire as, bursting through the inn door into the common room, she was met by the daunting scene of a smoke-filled hall crowded with Meltonians.

She came to an abrupt halt, her heart pounding from more than her recent exertions. One or two pairs of eyes turned to regard her with something approaching vague surprise, followed, it appeared, by a speculative interest. Soon she would undoubtedly be the cynosure of attention if she did not remove herself at once. It was only then, as the immensity of her new plight struck her, that she thought to let the hem of her skirts drop.

Nor was that all or the worst of it, she was soon to discover.

"Why, if it ain't Little Shpitfire," greeted her as she half-turned, searching for an alternate exit. "Been wondering if you would show up. 'Shpecially shince nobody sheems to know leasht little thing about hish lordship's upcoming nuptials."

To Francie's horror, she found herself face to face with Sir Fancy-Lace, no less besotted than the night before. The dolt, grinning maliciously, had the temerity to leer at her in a manner that could only be described as lewd and unspeakably familiar. What was more, he did not scruple to lay a hand on her. Grasp-

ing her rudely by the arm, he thrust her forward
toward the center of the room.

"Now that you're here, might as well shay hello to
your intended—*if*, that izh, you can pick him out of
the crowd."

Francie, having just made a harrowing escape from
the clutches of two murderous villains only to plunge
into a new bumblebroth of her own making, was in
no mood to tolerate the squire's boorish presence.
Suddenly, far from being intimidated by the oaf, she
dug her heels in and impaled him with a look that
would have flayed anyone less thick-witted than he.

"You may be sure I shall do more than that, sir, if
you do not instantly unhand me," she declared with
a haughtiness that would have done credit to Florence herself. Then, no doubt deeming it advisable to
demonstrate the truth of her threat and espying a
doorway that offered a means of escape, she did not
hesitate to bring the heel of her blue kid half-boot
down full force on the oaf's instep. The squire, letting
out a yelp, launched into a peculiar one-legged hop
while attempting to grasp his mistreated foot in his
hands.

Francie judged that, in the circumstances, retreat
was the better part of valor. Glancing back over her
shoulder at the squire, she darted through the gaping
doorway—and came up hard against an immovable
object.

"*Oh!*" she gasped, as a pair of strong arms swept
her into a crushing embrace. She was made instantly
and simultaneously aware that she was pinioned
against a hard chest, that her senses were being as-

sailed by the not unpleasing scents of tobacco and clean linen at exceedingly close range, and that, behind her, the squire had uttered a vengeful oath and was no doubt even then bolting after her. Still, having engaged in any number of wrestling matches with her brothers, she hardly considered herself at *point non plus*.

Francie prepared to resort to the only defense open to her.

"Cease and desist, madam," rumbled a deep, masculine voice, vibrant with wry amusement. The next instant firm hands set her a safe distance apart from her captor. "I beg your pardon, ma'am," she was coolly advised, "but I have a particular aversion to being kicked in the shin."

Startled, Francie glanced up into light, piercing eyes, lit just then with sardonic devils of laughter. She was given the further impression of strong, arrogant features rendered ruggedly handsome by dark, bristling eyebrows in a high, wide intelligent forehead, a long nose with a distinctly hawk-like cast to it, and a wide, sensitive mouth above a firm, stubborn chin. She knew him at once—the stranger from the hunt.

What came next happened with bewildering swiftness.

The squire burst through the doorway and came to a sliding halt.

"My Lord Ransome," he exclaimed, displaying every evidence of a man in the throes of some dread revelation.

The tall stranger lifted inquisitive eyebrows, and Francie launched herself against his chest.

Clasping her arms about his neck, she closed her eyes and, puckering her lips, lifted her face to his. "Well, my lord, what are you waiting for?" she demanded, when it seemed the proper response was not to be forthcoming. "Pray hurry, sir, and kiss me."

Harry Danvers pulled his horse up in the inn courtyard and, swinging down, thrust the reins into the hands of a stable lad.

"Walk him before bedding him," he ordered curtly and tossed the boy a coin before turning to make his way toward the entrance to the Pork Pie Inn.

"The devil," he muttered to himself, annoyed yet at having allowed himself to be persuaded to forego his usual rooms at the inn for an invitation to join Laverly's party at the viscount's hunting box. He might have known Lady Catherine would be there. There was nothing she could not persuade Laverly to do for her and little to which she would not stoop to have her own way. That she was set on having Harry back, he found not only unappealing but vastly unamusing. Their brief alliance had been a mistake from the very beginning, and he had not scrupled to disabuse her of the notion that anything could come of her misguided attempts to renew it.

Hell and the devil confound it, he cursed at the memory of the damnably uncomfortable evening spent warding off the raven-haired, green-eyed temptress. In the next breath he cursed himself for having been such a fool as to set aside the one rule that had served to preserve him from just such entanglements.

Not since his salad days, when he had succumbed to the manipulations of a scheming female with a heart of jade, had he allowed himself to set up so much as a light flirtation with a woman of gentle birth. Indeed, he much preferred the company of the less demanding creatures of the demimonde whose sole purpose was to ease a man's weightier existence. They, at least, knew the rules of the game, not the least of which was when an alliance was ended.

In Lady Catherine's case, he had made an exception only because she was a widow whose charm and elegance of style had momentarily blinded him to the fact that her wit was barbed and her manners naught but a camouflage for a spoiled disposition and a calculating nature, all of which had quickly palled on him. The affair had inevitably ended badly. Lady Catherine's vanity was hardly of the sort to brook any sort of denial, let alone one that had made her the talk of the Town.

Harry's lip curled in cynical self-derision. Indeed, he had long derived a deal of amusement from the fact that, having deliberately eschewed the society that had spawned him, he had made himself an object greatly to be desired. There was not a hostess ambitious of adding to her reputation who would not have viewed his presence at one of her balls, dinners, or galas as *un fait accompli*. In lieu of that, however, they were equally content to relegate him to the devil's domain. He was, in short, considered dangerous, a law unto himself, a rakeshame and a gambler whose sole redeeming virtues were a sizable fortune, a title, and an unattainability that could not but make him the prize Catch of the Marriage Mart.

That was the lure that had drawn Lady Catherine to set her cap for him. Certainly, he did not fool himself into believing it was for any deep affection she might have felt for him. Lady Catherine, he doubted not, was incapable of loving anyone, least of all any man who would not be ruled from his bed. And Harry, the product of a marriage of convenience that had never evolved beyond the formalities of producing an heir, entertained a distinct dislike of the notion of wedding in the absence of that particular emotion.

Not that any of that really signified, Harry told himself with a cynical twist of the lips. Matrimony, in any case, was the last thing he wished. Having yet to meet a female capable of engaging his interest for longer than it took to become intimately acquainted with her, he had come to believe that the woman did not exist who could break through his formidable defenses. Content, furthermore, to allow his cousin to inherit the title, he felt no particular urge to set up his nursery. There would seem, consequently, to be little reason to thrust himself into Parson's Mousetrap. He, after all, saw little to recommend in the notion of being legshackled for life to a female who would bore him hardly before the honeymooon was over.

Deliberately setting aside all thoughts of Lady Catherine and her most recent attempts to ensnare him, Harry entered the inn.

Due to the sizable sum he expended yearly to insure a room would always be available to him during
the meeting of the Quorn, he was greeted by the
innkeeper with a wide grin of welcome.

"Welcome back, my lord, to our humble establishment. You may be sure we have kept your rooms
ready and waiting for you. Shall I send a boy to fetch
your trunks in?"

"My trunks, along with my valet, I fear, will be de-
layed in arriving. You may send them up when they
do put in an appearance. In the meantime, I believe
a glass of your finest would not be amiss," he concluded, turning his steps toward the common room,
where, he doubted not, he would find any number
of his intimates engaged in drinking themselves under the table. Certainly there would be a game going
forth in one of the private rooms, which should offer
an agreeable means of passing a few hours, he mused,
as he came up to the doorway that led into the hall
crowded with not a few of the Meltonian set to which
he belonged.

What he did not expect was to be met with an immediate collision with a slender female who was obviously in a hurry.

It was purely instinctive to clasp his arms around
her to prevent her from falling. It was perhaps fortunate as well that he was possessed of quick reflexes.
Almost before his senses had time to register the intriguing fact that the small, lissome form conformed
to his larger frame in a most pleasing manner than
he became aware that his unwitting captive had lifted
a foot with obvious intentions.

Upon later reflection, it was to occur to him that not only had he been made the object of some malevolent and probably vengeful quirk of fate intent on teaching him the error of his ways, but he had taken firm leave of his senses. Hardly had he begun to congratulate himself on having preserved his shin from a punishing assault than he found himself clasped about the neck and staring down into eyes the spellbinding blue of sunlit pools of water and framed in a face that, tanned to a light golden brown, was as enchanting as it was lovely. It seemed, furthermore, that he was required for some unknown, but obviously pressing reason to kiss those lips offered up to him like ripe, rich cherries for the plucking.

A wry grin twitched at the corners of his mouth as it came to him that this ridiculous child, whoever she was, was an obvious innocent who had not the least notion what she was inviting. Then, abandoning all sense of rationale, Harry lowered his head and did precisely as he had been bidden.

Having kissed any number of women before, Harry was hardly a novice at that particular aspect of lovemaking. Still, it could not but occur to him a second or two later that he must be sadly slipping. Even taking into consideration the fact that he had, out of deference to her obvious youth and untutored innocence, restrained himself from all but the most circumspect of assaults on those lovely lips, he could not but be a trifle taken aback to discover the object of his efforts had one eye open and was peering at something apparently of far greater interest to her off to one side.

Now what the devil? he wondered, considerably humbled and not a little curious. Indeed, he could not but speculate that he was fast losing a grip on his sanity as he found himself in the peculiar position of trying with his lips still engaged to twist his head around in order to discover the object of the lady's attention.

The maneuver, while failing to reveal to him anything of a pertinent nature, at least served the purpose of reminding the young beauty of his presence. In mounting amusement, Harry beheld her lovely blue eye fix on his and hold, then in sudden and immediate consternation both eyes fly open to regard Harry with their complete and undivided awareness.

Only then, as imps of irrepressible mirth ignited unexpectedly in the intriguing blue depths of those orbs, did it occur to Harry that he had beheld many eyes of a captivating beauty, but never any to equal these. He was conscious of a sharp pang of disappointment as he felt the beguiling imp disengage her lips from his and pull hastily away.

"I-I beg your pardon, my lord," she gasped, revealing a countenance made lovelier still by the rosy blush on her cheeks. "But he is gone now. I believe it would be quite safe if you released me."

Harry, showing no immediate sign that he was in the least moved to comply with her request, merely tightened his arm more snugly about her waist. "Do you? And what if I were to say I have no intention of unloosing my hold on you until I may be sure you will not instantly fly away? I believe, my dear, that you at least owe me an explanation."

If he had expected by this to impress her with the enormity of her actions in flinging herself at a complete stranger, he was soon to discover he had fallen far short of his mark.

To his amazement, rather than betraying the smallest alarm or even a modicum of outrage at this pronouncement, the little baggage had the temerity to smile up at him with what gave every evidence of her unmitigated trust.

"You may be sure that I am well aware of what I owe you, my lord, not the least of which is my unutterable relief at discovering my reputation is safe in your hands. I am only amazed that I did not realize at once who you were, when I first saw you this afternoon. I should have saved myself a great deal of worry over nothing."

"Should you, indeed?" murmured Harry, who not only had not the least notion what the devil she was talking about, but could only marvel that any female who knew him by reputation, as this one claimed to do, would choose to comfort herself with the knowledge that her good name somehow depended on him.

"You know very well that I should," retorted that intriguing young woman. "It is simply not in your nature, after all, to betray a lady's trust. I daresay you understood perfectly why I took that jump."

"Oh, perfectly," agreed Harry, suddenly considerably enlightened. He might have known she would be the young daredevil who had had the audacity to insert herself into the midst of that august gathering of top of the trees Meltonians. There surely could not have been another like her in the sparse population that comprised Melton Mowbray. "I daresay you were overcome by what amounted to an irresistible temptation."

"Impulse, my lord," corrected the minx, grinning in perfect accord. "Papa says it is my one besetting sin, and I daresay he is right. It is undoubtedly what landed me in my present predicament, though I really cannot think how I should have foreseen that a mere stroll on the terrace would lead me to overhear two murderous villains plotting against my sister's husband or that, in consequence of my being discovered, I should be forced to flee for my life straight into the odious person of Sir Fancy-Lace. You do see that I had little choice but to avail myself of your protection, do you not?"

"Oh, indubitably," agreed Harry, who did not see at all how he had come to be embroiled in what gave every promise of being just the sort of bumblebroth he had always taken great pains to avoid. No doubt it was a last, primal instinct of self-preservation that prompted him to remove his arm without further preamble from around the alluringly slender waist. "It does occur to me to wonder, however, why you chose this particular fashion of eliciting it. At the risk of seeming obtuse, Miss—er—Miss . . ."

"Powell, my lord," supplied that worthy with an unsettling readiness. "Lady Francine Elizabeth Powell, though I vastly prefer Francie."

"Yes, I should suppose you would," Harry reflected, beginning to grasp a great deal about the impulsive Lady Powell, not the least of which was the fact that, besides being a complete and utter hoyden, she would seem to have a total absence of qualms about involving a stranger in whatever harebrained toil she had got herself in. An alarm sounded in his brain, and every instinct urged him to instantly remove himself from her presence.

It was, consequently, with a sense of having totally abandoned all sense of reason that he heard himself asking the fatal question: "Why a kiss, Lady Powell? Your impulsive nature aside, surely it must have occurred to you that such a ploy might be just a trifle in the extreme?"

"Not at all, my lord," was the immediate response, made all the more startling by the smile of unruffled composure with which it was accompanied. "How else should I have convinced Sir Fancy-Lace I was telling the truth about us?"

Harry stared at the lovely countenance with a distinctly fixed expression. "How else indeed?" he observed, stricken by a sudden and mind-numbing sense of foreboding. "Er—what truth is that, Lady Powell?"

He was not in the least comforted to note that Lady Powell demonstrated for the first time a vague uneasiness in his presence.

"Are you quite sure you wish to know, my lord?" she queried, eyeing him doubtfully. "I daresay you might not like it, though, as a soldier, you must see I was left very little choice in the matter. Especially when I tell you I was convinced Sir Fancy-Lace, like the dark Lord of Bartleby Castle who entertained foul designs against Lady Hortensia, was fully capable of breaking into my rooms last night. Besides, it was not really a lie. After all, as a child I did promise that one day I should marry the man who had saved Phillip's life at grave risk to his own. It was a silly, girlish fantasy, I own, one which, you will be glad to know, I have long since outgrown. I am well aware I am sadly lacking in any feminine accomplishments that would make me a likely candidate for a man's attentions. Besides which, I have not the least wish ever to be legshackled.''

Harry, who, besides having a deal of difficulty making any sense of Lady Powell's convoluted explanation, could only be relieved that he was unable to recall any heroic incidents involving himself and an alleged Phillip, took little comfort in the imp's final avowal. As a man of no little experience in the world, he knew well how little one could rely on a woman's stated aversion to matrimony, especially one with Lady Powell's obvious attributes. Short of entering a nunnery, there was not one chance in a thousand the young beauty would end up a spinster on the shelf. It remained only to take steps to insure he was not made the dupe in what would appear to be a well-contrived plot devised for that very purpose.

"It would seem, Lady Powell, that you are to be congratulated on your resourcefulness. Indeed, I believe I am almost moved to pity your poor unsuspecting squire. On the other hand, you may be certain that I should never prove so easy a mark," he added with a steely edged softness that had served in the past to deflate the pretensions of any number of simpering females and their matchmaking mamas.

It soon became apparent, however, that he had

failed to take the measure of Lady Francine Elizabeth Powell.

She awarded him a beaming look of approval. "I *knew* you would understand. Phillip said he could ask for no better man to have at his back in a donnybrook fair. And then, too, one must take into account your adventurous nature. I believe, sir, we are two of a kind in that respect. And now I shall wish you goodnight, my lord," she added, favoring him with a smile that was as disarming as it was utterly guileless. "And thank you. Though I daresay we shall not meet again, you may be sure I shall never forget you."

She was halfway up the first flight of stairs before it occurred to Harry that she had yet to answer his original question.

"Er—Lady Powell," he said, gazing up at her. "No doubt you will pardon my curiosity, but I cannot but wonder. What was it, precisely, that you told the besotted squire?"

The young beauty did not even pause in her climb up the staircase. "Nothing to signify, my lord," she flung lightly over her shoulder. "Only that I was sworn to wed your lordship."

The next instant she was gone, having vanished around the corner, leaving Harry to stare after her with a peculiarly frozen aspect.

Four

"Really, Flo," said Francie, gazing doubtfully down from her elevated position on a stool in the middle of her sister's drawing room at Florence's coiffed curls and frowning countenance. "Are you *quite* certain Papa said he would stand the nonsense? If we continue in this vein, I daresay we shall soon land him on the rocks."

"I wish you will not be absurd." Florence stood back to study the effect of her younger sister in pale lavender. "I have never been more certain of anything. Papa gave me *carte blanche* in providing you with what you will need. And since we are starting practically from scratch, we must of necessity purchase at least half a dozen of everything. You may be sure it is nothing to signify. It is hardly likely Papa will be forced to sell out of the funds. Now pray stand still and stop fretting. The lavender vigonia is absolutely stunning on you."

Francie eyed askance her image in the ormolu looking glass. In the two weeks since her arrival in London, she had done little more than stand on a stool in her silk underthings while patterns and bolts

of cloth were held up to her. She had been pinned
and prodded and scrutinized until she had come to
the point of contemplating open rebellion if she had
to undergo one more hour of fittings. At least, she
reflected with a sigh, they had progressed to trying
on finished gowns.

Madame du Mauvier, the modiste Florence favored, had arrived that morning with three morning
dresses, two walking gowns, a rust velvet riding habit,
two ball gowns, and no fewer than three evening
dresses. Clearly, the woman had kept her entire force
of seamstresses at work round the clock to have
achieved such a feat, Francie marveled.

The outcome was equally impressive, she decided,
willing to concede that, when it came to matters of
fashion, she could not have asked for a better mentor
than Florence. Francie could hardly believe the elegant young woman in the looking glass was the same
Francine Elizabeth Powell who had left Greensward
for London certain that she was fated to join the
ranks of the wallflowers. Certainly, she had never
looked less like the tomboy who had been used to
engage in rough and tumble games with her twin
brothers.

The lavender vigonia in question was a round gown
cut in the Empire with puffed sleeves tapering at the
elbows to embroidered wrist bands. Light and flowing, it accentuated her slender form while drawing
subtle attention to her feminine curves, Francie was
quick to note.

She could not but notice as well that her enforced
stay indoors, coupled as it had been with daily appli-

cations of a cucumber lotion, had served to rid her cheeks of their unfashionable tan. She was left with what could only be described as an interesting pallor, which would have delighted her oldest sister Lucy no end. No doubt the budding novelist would have instantly concocted a tale of romantic adventure involving Francie in a blighted *affaire de coeur* that had resulted in her having experienced an exquisite anguish of some sort. All of which was patently ridiculous when one considered that Francie was never allowed to go anywhere except shopping in Bond Street or to silly teas attended only by girls her own age and their doting mamas.

Equally frustrating to Francie was the fact that, thus far, Florence had proven uncommonly stubborn in her refusal to admit there was anything the least peculiar about her husband's frequent and lengthy absences from the four-story house on Grosvenor Square. As it was, Leighton had not put in an appearance once since Francie's arrival at her sister's.

"You must understand, Francine," Flo would inevitably reply in answer to Francie's attempts to question her, "Leighton is a man of many responsibilities. His holdings and various business enterprises occupy a great deal of his time."

All of which was patent nonsense, Francie reflected, giving Flo's trim figure garbed in pale rose an assessing glance. Leighton employed any number of people to see to his interests. He was hardly required to spend his entire time doing what he paid others to do. Besides which, he would seem to have plenty of leisure to devote to the mysterious Madame

Noire, if what Francie had overheard that night at the inn was true.

More significant, however, than any of these other arguments against Florence's insistence that nothing was amiss in her marriage was the air of preternatural calm which she had taken to wearing rather like an impregnable coat of armor against the world. Francie had not spent seventeen years in the company of her sister without having come to know when Flo was behaving in a manner wholly inconsistent with her true nature.

In the norm, one might sooner have expected pigs to fly than to look for Florence Anne Marie Powell to present an unflappability that nothing could shake—not even Francie's avowal she would rather parade naked in Hyde Park than consent to wearing stays or anything so barbarous as a leather bust improver beneath her gowns. It was obvious to Francie that her sister was in even deeper waters than she had previously imagined.

Indeed, for the first time in their life-long relationship, Francie was moved to regret that she was not on more intimate terms with her sister. Still, she supposed there were other ways of discovering what Leighton was about. What she needed was to meet people outside of her considerably restricted circle, something which Florence's strategy of introducing her charge gradually into Society in order to give Francie time to adjust to her new environs had thus far made utterly impossible.

As it was, she had managed to make only one acquaintance who moved in the sort of circles in which one might have learned the kind of information that Francie required, and he was hardly the sort to whom the propriety-conscious Florence would have given her approval. Not that that would have, in the norm, stopped Francie. The truth was she had not the least notion how one went about contacting a man who made it a practice to avoid all the sorts of fashionable events to which she was restricted. An irrepressible grin tugged at her lips at the thought of Ransome at a tea for young ladies. No doubt his mere appearance would have been enough to scatter the entire company.

All except for herself, of course, she temporized as she dutifully turned on the stool in order for Madame du Mauvier to make adjustments to the hem of the gown. Francie would have liked very well to see the elusive nobleman again. Indeed, he had occupied an inordinate share of her ruminations since their encounter at the inn in Melton Mowbray. Not that she entertained any illusions that he had given her so much as a thought in the interim. Indeed, he had very likely forgotten all about her, she decided with an unconscious moue of regret. He was Ransome, after all. She doubted not that he was probably used to having any number of females fling themselves at him.

Still, if the opportunity should by some miracle present itself, she was quite certain she could contrive a way to remind him of their brief encounter. She was fully confident the man who had heroically rescued Phillip would not only be willing but more than able to help her discover the identity of the mysterious

Madame Noire. Indeed, she could not but berate herself for not having had the presence of mind to question him on that very subject when she had had him
so conveniently on hand. But then she had, upon
reflection, to admit she had not been wholly herself
at the time. After all, she had not only just effected
a harrowing escape from two murderous villains, a
room full of Meltonians, and the besotted squire, but
she had experienced her very first kiss from a gentleman, as well. And not just any gentleman at that,
she reminded herself with a wholly impish smile, but
the Earl of Ransome himself.

Her one regret was that she had been so preoccupied with such extraneous matters as the possibility
of being fallen upon by her pursuers or further in-
sulted by the squire that she had quite utterly failed
to derive the full effect from the experience.

Indeed, far from rendering her trembling and weak
as the heroines in her sister Lucy's tales of romance,
her first and only kiss had left her feeling distinctly
foolish and not a little disgusted with herself. At its
inception, she had been ridiculously distracted, and
at its end, she had been far too embarrassed at having
been caught with one eye open to notice very much
about the kiss itself. Still, she could not deny having
sustained a decided jolt upon becoming suddenly and
irrevocably aware of the man himself. Nor could she
be insensible of the fact that her whole being became
suffused with a wholly disturbing warmth whenever
she recalled the incident.

What a fool she was, she chided herself, to have
wasted what could only be described as a momentous

opportunity. The last thing she might have expected was to find herself in the embrace of the man who, having long ago captured her imagination, had figured in her girlish fantasies of romance and adventure. It was simply too ridiculous that she had not properly been paying attention at what should have been the supreme moment of realization of a dream too good to come true. And now she found herself doomed always to wonder what, exactly, she had so inopportunely missed! Really, it was the height of absurdity, she thought.

"Francie," accused Florence, fortuitously choosing just then to break in on her sister's unrewarding thoughts, "I do wish you will pay attention when I am talking to you. I daresay you have not heard a word I said. Are you quite all right? I might expect woolgathering from Lucy, but hardly from you."

"I was not woolgathering," declared Francie, brought to an instant awareness that, not only had the modiste taken herself off, but Florence was regarding her with a quizzical frown in her blue-violet eyes. Frantically, she tried to recall the threads of her sister's words. She had vaguely heard something about a Miss Wilmington and Hyde Park. Now, what the devil had one to do with the other? she wondered.

"Oh, very well," she admitted grudgingly, unable to resolve the conundrum, "I was not paying attention. I was thinking how if I were home, I should be having a cracking good ride just about now instead of standing on a stool in a dress I shall probably never be allowed to wear anywhere other than to some silly tea party that I shall find exceedingly boring."

Francie, observing Florence's lips, which one moonstruck young gentleman had been moved to compare to the "unfolding petals of a blushing rose," go ominously white, steeled herself for one of her sister's distempered freaks.

"You may choose to poke bogey at me if you wish," Florence replied stiffly. "Indeed, I am no doubt sorry that you find little to recommend in meeting young ladies who belong to the best families. I'm sure it never occurred to you that by attending all those tea parties you so thoroughly detest you are accumulating a sizable acquaintanceship. Nor have you ever once stopped to think that, when you do go to your first ball, you will not find yourself all alone in a room full of complete strangers. I suggest, Francie, that it will be a comfort to you to discover you are in the company of any number of girls your own age with whom you may exchange confidences. I know in your place I should have done."

Francie, who indeed had never once considered the possibility that her sister might have a good reason for subjecting them both to an endless round of parties made up solely of young girls (other than to impel Francie to improve her deplorable lack of social skills), felt rather as if she had just been landed a facer. She was given for the first time to see what it must have been like for Florence, thrust into Society without a single acquaintance other than Lucy, who had, when one came right down to it, been very little more experienced than Flo herself. Even for the acknowledged Beauty of the family, it must have been a daunting experience.

"The devil, Flo," Francie blurted, scrambling down from the stool to face her sister. "Why did you never tell anyone? You may be sure Mama would have seen to it that you were properly introduced had she the least inkling how it was. And, poor Lucy. How dreadful she would feel if she knew she had failed to do all in her power to make your come-out as painless as possible. I daresay she assumed you would just naturally know how to go on."

"I wish you will not be absurd, Francie," Florence protested snappishly. "Of course Lucy did everything one could possibly ask—more, in fact. She exerted every effort to make sure there was not a door closed to me."

"Then, what the deuce are we talking about?" demanded Francie, who could not but be aware Florence was being deliberately evasive.

"Had you been attending, you would know, Francie. As it happens, I was telling you Miss Wilmington of the Sussex Wilmingtons has condescended to invite you to stroll with her this afternoon along the Broad Walk at the fashionable hour of five."

"Gammon! We were discussing you and Lucy, and I'll be dashed if I'll let you change the subject. For once in your life, Flo, I wish you will talk to me as if I were not some distant acquaintance you would not in the norm give the time of day."

A distinct flush colored Florence's cheeks at the unexpected outburst from her sister. Rather abruptly she turned her back on Francie.

"*Must* you use language better suited to the stable?" she demanded, reaching down to gather up a pile of pattern books scattered about on the cherry-wood occasional table. "You have no idea how ruinous it can be for a young girl in her first Season to be thought common and ill-bred. And that is precisely how you will be judged if you forget yourself even once in the presence of company."

Francie, who had not failed to note the flicker of a shadow in her sister's eyes just before Florence averted her face, suffered an unfamiliar pang of guilt. The devil, she thought, troubled not by her sister's reprimand, which she had deliberately invited, but by the off-handed manner in which it had been delivered. Faith, she and Flo had engaged in verbal fencing matches for as long as Francie could remember, and, while Flo might present a prim and proper exterior, she had never lacked a quick and ready tongue. Flo had always delivered as good as she got.

It was, in fact, as unlike Florence Anne Marie Powell to refuse to take the bait when it was offered, as it was for Francine to wish to hear her sister read her one of her curtain lectures. And yet that was precisely what Francie found herself thinking—that she would have liked nothing better than to see Florence kick up a dust. At least that would have been the Florence Francie knew.

Still, there was more than one way to skin a cat, Francie reflected, studying Florence with pursed lips. Perhaps it was time she tried a different approach.

"I am sorry, Flo. Indeed, I am sure I beg your pardon," Francie ventured, surprised to discover that she meant it. "You are right, of course. I do have a frightful habit of speaking whatever comes to my mind."

Florence's head came around, her lovely eyes wary. With a wry grin, Francie shrugged. "Well, I do," she said. "And pray do not try to deny it. After all, you have been telling me as much for simply ages."

"But I have no intention of denying it. Your language can be deplorable." Flo stopped. Unexpectedly, the perfectly arched eyebrows drew together over the equally perfect nose. "Have I really been so bad as all that?"

"As all what?" Francie countered, startled by the sudden change in subject.

Florence gave an impatient gesture of the hand. "You know very well what," she snapped, only to immediately catch herself. Drawing a long breath, she squared her shoulders with seeming resolution. "I am aware that we have never been particularly close, Francie," she began again in carefully modulated tones, "but I had hoped you entertained at least a modicum of affection for me. We are sisters, after all. If I have seemed overly critical, it is only because I want more than anything to—well, to save you from making a mull of your first Season the—the way I did," she finished on a strangled note. At last she turned to Francine. "Is that so very wrong of me, Francie?"

"Fiddle!" ejaculated Francie, considerably taken aback at the tremor in her sister's voice. "I never thought to hear you talk such twaddle. Naturally, I am moderately fond of you, even if you are a terrible nag. I might even go so far as to say there are times when I am actually glad to have you as my sister."

At this somewhat mixed declaration of affection, Florence turned rueful eyes on Francie. "Repellent brat. I suppose I asked for that."

"But of course you did, stupid," Francie said, grinning back at Flo. "If you weren't behaving like an utter peagoose, you would know that you do not have to ask for my affection. We are Powells, and Powells— even when we cannot agree on the simplest thing— always stick together. Can you think for one moment you would have allowed Mama to foist me on you—or vice-versa, for that matter—if that were not the case?"

A stricken look darkened Florence's eyes as abruptly she turned away. "If only I could believe that," she said in a voice little above a whisper. "You cannot know how I . . ."

Francie caught her breath as she waited for Florence to complete that poignant outburst.

"But no matter." Coming about, Flo summoned a smile. "Whatever you might think, Francie, I assure you I have never considered your coming here in the light of having you 'foisted' on me. I could not be more pleased that Mama trusted me to bring you out. Or happier to have you with me, for that matter. I confess I have been a trifle lonely of late."

"Well, and who wouldn't be," Francie answered, bracingly, aware that Flo had ever so slightly relaxed the barrier between them. "I daresay London is not half so lively as Greensward used to be when everyone was still at home. You would hardly know the place these days. With you and Lucy gone and the twins away at school, it is as quiet as a churchyard. Instead of trying to marry me off, which is at best a lost cause, you would do better to look for someone for Will. What Greensward needs is a whole new batch of Powells to bring it back to life."

Francie pronounced this last with such conviction that Florence was startled into a helpless gurgle of laughter. "Really, Francie, you are utterly hopeless. Can you imagine Will's face if he heard you plotting to marry him off for the sole purpose of replenishing the diminishing population at Greensward? Why, you make him sound little better than a stud horse."

"I daresay he would not mind being thought a stud," reflected Francie unrepentantly. "Very likely it would only boost his male pride. Not that he needs a boost. Ever since Lady Inglethorpe maneuvered him into the garden with the obvious intent of winning a declaration from him, he has come to think of himself as practically irresistible to women. It was lucky for him Mama saw them from the Summer Room and guessed what Lady Inglethorpe was about, else he would be legshackled even now to a widow with two aspiring daughters."

"Oh!" gasped Florence, clasping Francie's hands in mingled horror and delight. "You cannot mean it. Lady Inglethorpe is five and twenty, if she is a day. And quite without a feather to fly with besides. Still, she is thought to be uncommonly well to look upon. No doubt Will may be excused for his lapse in judgment."

"And how not, my dear," observed a new, masculine voice from the doorway in unmistakably acerbic accents. "It would seem to be a common enough failing among those of my gender."

At this pronouncement, both women turned to be met with the sight of a gentleman, who, though of average height, was well-knit and powerfully built. Lounging with one shoulder propped against the doorframe, he presented a compelling picture of manhood.

A mirthless smile twitched at the masculine lips at Florence's startled exclamation of "My lord!" accompanied as it was with Francie's simultaneous and undeniably delighted cry of "Paul!"

"Quite so," noted Paul Moberly, Marquis of Leighton, as Florence's complexion went from pearl to rose, then white again. "My dear," he murmured, dropping a light buss on Florence's cheek. "It would seem nothing has changed in my absence," he added, taking a moment to study his wife's curiously frozen expression. "Except," he amended as he turned to clasp Francie's hands in both of his own, "I have the good fortune to be met by *two* beautiful women. Francie Powell, I should hardly have known you. You fair take my breath away."

"You may be sure that I hardly recognize myself," admitted that worthy, laughing as she gaily dipped him a curtsey. "I owe it all to Flo, who is determined to make a proper lady of me—never mind that it is quite utterly hopeless."

"You, my dearest Francie, are already perfection personified," declared Leighton, taking in the lively young face turned up to his. "I should not change a thing. If anything, I find I almost pity the poor, unsuspecting males who have not the least notion what is about to descend into their midst."

"I daresay they are perfectly safe," Francie retorted, wrinkling her nose ingenuously up at him. "You, sir, however, are in danger of earning my disapprobation. I should almost think you have been deliberately avoiding me. Here I have been in London for all of two weeks, and all Flo can tell me is that you are occupied with your many responsibilities. I confess I had thought you would be glad to see me."

"And so I am," Leighton replied without missing a beat. "I regret I was not here to welcome you on your arrival. As it happens, I was unavoidably kept away."

"Fiddle," ejaculated Francie, studying the stern, baffling countenance with rueful eyes. Faith, the man was as close as Florence and every whit as stubborn. What they both needed was a decided jolt, and who better than herself to administer it? "Still, I suppose I must forgive you. Now that you are here, however, you must know that I depend on you to persuade Flo to allow me a gallop in Hyde Park. And pray do not tell me it is wholly unacceptable behavior. I am not so green as not to know that I should be perfectly safe at an unfashionably early morning hour—if I have an escort. Do please say you will, Paul. I have not had Jester out since I arrived in London."

Having delivered that little fly in the ointment, Francie stepped innocently back to await developments. They were not long in coming.

Florence's frozen aspect underwent an almost instantaneous transformation, from preternatural calm to unmistakable horror. "I am afraid that is quite impossible, Francie," Florence hastily interjected. "It would only be inviting trouble. If you must ride out, I suggest we go in the carriage."

"The carriage, my dear?" murmured Leighton, his dark eyes inscrutable behind drooping eyelids as they came to rest on his wife. "I was under the impression your sister was a bruising rider."

Florence appeared most uncharacteristically to flinch beneath that probing gaze. "She is, of course. I have seldom seen her equal on a horse. And that is the problem. She has been used at home to ride with complete abandon. What is acceptable in the North Yorks, however, will hardly serve in Hyde Park."

"Really, Flo, you cannot think I am such a gaby as to jump the hedges or ride neck or nothing in full sight of anyone who happens along," Francie protested, thinking to help matters along. "If you cannot trust me to keep my head, you might at least allow that Paul would never forget what is owed the proprieties. One would almost believe you doubt he can keep me in line."

"Well, my dear?" queried his lordship with one quizzically elevated eyebrow. "I confess I am curious to hear your response."

"I-I wish you will not be absurd—either of you," uttered Florence, suffering a distinct crack in her composure. "Of course I have complete confidence in you, Paul. It is only that you do not know my sister as I do. Francie has an absolute knack for landing herself in trouble."

"And I, I must assume by extension, am unequal to the task of preventing such an occurrence," extrapolated the marquis, seemingly little amused at such a conclusion. "Ironic, really, when one considers I am accounted a man of not inconsiderable influence among my peers."

Florence's face assumed a stricken expression, which, had it not been just the sort of reaction Francie had been hoping for, would have caused that worthy a pang of remorse. "But that is not at all what I meant, Paul," Florence declared. "You know it was not. You must know I hold you in the highest esteem."

"Do I, Florence, my love?" Leighton's hand beneath her chin compelled her to look at him. A baffled look passed over his stern features, to be as quickly hidden. The next moment his hand dropped. "But then, if you say so, of course I must. It would seem, my dear, that we find ourselves once more at *point-non-plus*. At least I should be gratified that you have at last thought to remember my name, not once, but twice, as it were. As to the other matter, much as I should like to take you riding in Hyde Park, Francie, I fear circumstances make it quite impossible."

"You are going away again," Florence said at once, her head coming up.

"I am really afraid I must, my dear. But then, I daresay you will hardly notice I am gone. It is the Season, after all, and you have Francie to bring out. You will both be far too busy with an endless round of engagements to miss me. I should undoubtedly be quite *de trop*."

It was on Francie's tongue to declare that he should be a deal worse than that if he could so heartlessly abandon them for the doubtlessly more scintillating company of the mysterious Madame Noire. The look on Florence's face, however, quite robbed her of speech. The next instant, announcing he had just come for a few of his things, Leighton had turned and sauntered from their presence.

"Esteem? Good God, Flo," Francie exploded, collapsing in the wingchair next to the Adams' fireplace. "Surely you could come up with something just a trifle less daunting. For heaven's sake, he is your husband, whom, I might add, you have not seen for some considerable time."

Florence, jarred from her frozen stance, pierced Francie through with a glance. "What can you possibly know of it!" she cried. "You cannot know what it is to be married to a man who cannot bear the sight of you. Pray God that you never do!" she ended on a strangled note and, gathering up her skirts, bolted from the room.

"Flo!" Francie called after her, springing to her feet. "Flo, for heaven's sake, I didn't mean to—"

Five

The devil, thought Francie, sinking back into the chair. That had certainly gone well, had it not, she reflected wryly, dropping her chin on one elbow.

It had been immediately apparent from the moment Leighton arrived on the scene that a great deal had gone awry in what had begun as a promising alliance. Florence had suddenly given every appearance of one freshly dipped in starch, while Leighton had worn the wary aspect of a man confronted by an insoluble and potentially painful conundrum. It had not taken Francie more than a moment or two to see that what was needed was for the two to sit down and simply talk to one another. Obviously, such a rational solution had failed to suggest itself to the marquis and marchioness, however. Judging from the manner in which they had parted, *they* seemed determined on a ruinous course based on a mutual assumption of irreconcilable differences.

Still, perhaps all was not yet lost, thought Francie, never one to give up in the face of adversity. Leighton and Florence had been happy together at the beginning, she was sure of it. Surely their feelings had not so completely altered that they could not rediscover what they once had. The thing was to contrive a way to make Flo and Leighton stay together in one place long enough to allow their natural inclinations to come to the fore. Not an impossible task—unless, of course, she thought, recalling the two villains outside the Pork Pie Inn, Leighton ruined everything by cutting his stick before the thing was done.

Francie's eyes glittered at the memory of that overheard conversation. Madame Noire, whoever she was, was hardly the sort one would wish to have at one's back. Indeed, Francie wondered if Leighton could truly be so enamored as to be oblivious to that pertinent facet of the woman's character. In the norm, Francie would have accounted him a man of no little intellect. But then, very often in matters of this sort, intellect would seem to be strangely suspended, she reflected, calling to mind Lucy's *Lady in Waiting,* or *The Skeleton in the Castle Dungeon,* in which Lady Gwendolyn had been blinded by overweening passion to Sir William Desmond's cold and calculating nature. Unfortunately, there was not a daring Captain Clairmont available to reveal to Leighton the true character of the object of his obsession. There was only herself.

The devil, thought Francie, acutely aware how utterly useless it would be for her to try to warn Leighton of his peril. The last thing he would wish to discuss with his wife's younger sister was the sinister character of one who was very likely his paramour. And even if he could be brought to listen to her, he was hardly likely to place the least reliance on any-

thing she had to say on the subject. She, after all, was
only a green girl who had yet to make her curtsey in
polite Society. She was not supposed to even know
such creatures existed, let alone that her brother-in-
law was apparently keeping company with such a one.
The most she could expect was to earn his anger and
at the very least his demand to know where she had
come up with such an outlandish notion, and that
was the very last thing she could wish.

She counted herself singularly fortunate that thus
far not a word of her most recent plunge into iniquitous waters had reached London, a circumstance
which she did not doubt she owed to the Earl of Ransome's rare integrity. Not that she had been in the
least worried, she told herself. As a man of honor,
after all, it would hardly occur to Ransome to betray
a lady's trust. Still, the entire sequence of events, cul-
minating in her rescue from the besotted squire by
Ransome, had all been a matter of luck, and Francie,
ever of a practical nature, was perfectly aware that
she would be exceedingly foolish to trust her fate to
anything so fickle as Dame Fortune.

She would vastly prefer to let sleeping dogs lie than
risk everything by revealing to Leighton how she had
come to learn about Madame Noire. *He,* after all,
could hardly be depended upon to look with tolerance upon the circumstance of her having publicly
compromised herself with a notorious rakeshame in
the unprepossessing surrounds of an inn. Very likely
he would see fit to go straight to her dearest Papa,
who would have no other recourse but to demand
Ransome do the right thing by his daughter—and

that she could not allow. She would rather suffer ruination than submit to marry a man who could not possibly want her for his wife. Indeed, she would never have been able to forgive herself for taking undue advantage of the earl's generosity.

All of which left her with very little choice in the matter. Leighton must be saved, and only she could do it. If she could not depend on luck, she must make her own opportunities, and the very first order of business was to contrive to steal from the house without Florence in attendance.

It was at that point that her thoughts were rudely interrupted by the clang of the knocker belowstairs, followed moments later by the appearance at the withdrawing room door of Reynolds, the marquis's exceedingly superior butler.

"I beg your pardon, Lady Francine, but there is a gentleman caller below who desires to see you," Reynolds announced, extending a salver upon which resided a calling card.

"Me, Reynolds?" inquired Francie, as she reached for the card. "Are you quite certain?"

"His lordship was most specific, m'lady. He inquired if Lady Francine Elizabeth Powell was home to visitors. I have shown him into the Rose Room. How do you wish me to reply?"

"How?" Francie stared at the card. The name printed in bold Gothic sans-serif seemed to leap up at her. *Ransome.* Good God. It would seem that luck had not, after all, abandoned her!

Instantly her head came up. "Why, that I shall be down directly," she said, her smile suddenly dazzling.

"And, Reynolds, you need not bother informing my sister of the earl's arrival. I shall go and tell her myself."

"As you wish, m'lady," intoned the butler, backing out of the room.

Hardly had the door shut behind Reynolds before Francie was reaching behind her to undo the pearl fastenings at the back of her gown. If Leighton had come home only to gather up a few things that he needed, she had very little time.

Harry stood, hands clasped behind his back, and stared out the window overlooking Grosvenor Square. Watching the Countess of Shayle depart in her carriage pulled by a showy pair of greys, not to mention a pair of nannies walking their young charges on leading strings, he found himself asking, not for the first time, how the devil he had ended up here. Only a fortnight past, he had been counting himself exceedingly fortunate to have eluded unscathed what had given every promise of being an inescapable entanglement, and now what must he do but pursue the dragon to its lair.

A wry smile twisted at the handsome lips as an image, not of a fire-breathing monster, but of an impish face framed in hair the color of spun gold and graced with eyes the brilliance of sapphires sparkling with glints of laughter, rose up to haunt him. And haunt him, it had, like the most pertinacious of ghosts, wrecking his sleep and distracting him from his various waking pursuits.

Damn the chit! Given the tantalizing tidbits of a puzzle the troublesome imp had left him with, it would have been marvelous, indeed, had he *not* found himself worrying over them like a cursed dog with a bone. Having culled his brain for a se'ennight and made extensive inquiries, he had finally convinced himself that, far from numbering a lord of Bartleby Castle, or a Lady Hortensia among his acquaintances, no such personages had ever existed. Furthermore, although he had effected any number of narrow escapes while on the Continent, he was reasonably sure none had involved the heroic rescue of anyone named Phillip.

Having come at last to the conclusion that either the ridiculous child was a consummate liar or she had mistaken him for someone else, he should have been content to let the matter rest. Unfortunately, he could not shake the conviction that in one thing she had been telling the truth.

She had most certainly overheard *something* at the inn that had sent her into a flight, and, if indeed it involved a murderous plot, then she was undoubtedly in grave risk of her life.

It had been with a wry sense of unreality that he had found himself making discreet inquiries into the existence of a noble branch of a family bearing the name Powell. That it had led him at last to an Earl of Bancroft of Greensward in the North York Moors had only been marginally helpful. Lady Francine had been traveling south, undoubtedly to make her come-out in London. Subsequent inquiries had revealed that, while the Earl of Bancroft did indeed own a Town House on London's Portman Square, he had let it out to a Mr. Horace Milkcross for the Season.

Harry had come to an impasse, a circumstance which should have relieved him of any further responsibility toward the chit. After all, he had made an effort to locate her. It was, consequently, with a sense of having abandoned all rationale, not to mention his acute instinct for self-preservation, that Harry had found himself that morning at a wholly uncivilized hour on the road to Brighton to visit his esteemed mama, the countess.

No doubt it was the measure of his growing preoccupation with the elusive Lady Powell that he had broken yet another of his ironclad rules on her behalf. Certainly, prior to that fateful night when Lady Francine Elizabeth Powell had seen fit to hurl herself into his arms, upsetting the previously even tenor of his life, not to mention his equilibrium, he had not felt the smallest compulsion to place himself within twenty miles of his mama's proximity.

In retrospect, he could not be certain who was more taken aback, himself or the countess, upon finding themselves face to face across the drawing room. He had not the least doubt, however, who derived the most enjoyment out of it.

"Harry, by all that is marvelous," had been the countess's fond greeting to her only son, "I daresay you are the last person I should have expected to pop up on my doorstep. And how like you not to bother to send a warning ahead that you were coming."

"But how not, Mother?" Harry had returned smoothly. "I had no wish to arrive only to find you had another engagement elsewhere. As it happens I had a particular desire to catch you at home to visitors."

"Harumph!" declared his mama, taking in her son's tall, imposing figure with a baleful glance. "Same old Harry."

Harry bent indolently at the waist in acquiescence. "Naturally, I should not wish to disappoint you. How have you been, Mother?"

"Well enough, thank you," she informed him, as she uncompromisingly settled her trim figure, becomingly garbed in a gown of rose cassenette, on the dimity sofa. "Not that you would care one way or another. As it happens, I have every expectation of living to see the title go to your Cousin Bertie."

"You cannot know how relieved I am to hear it," said Harry. Following his mother's example, he dropped negligently into a caffoy covered wing chair, his long legs, crossed at the ankles, stretched carelessly out before him.

His mama's aristocratic lips thinned ever so slightly at sight of him.

Harry smiled charmingly.

"What is it that you want from me, Harry?" the countess flatly demanded, her curiosity no doubt having gotten the better of her. "Since I dare not hope that you have come to inform me you have decided at long last to set up your nursery, I cannot imagine what we should have to say to one another."

"No less can I, Mother, save that I know how vast is your knowledge of the noble families of the realm. As it happens, I am interested in discovering where the

Earl of Bancroft's daughter might put up while in Town."

"Bancroft? Now, why the devil should you wish to know that, Harry? I am aware of only two daughters by the earl, both of them married—one, as it happens, to the Duke of Lathrop."

"Lathrop? Good God," exclaimed Harry, startled out of his usual *sang-froid*. If Lathrop was the target of a plot to cut his stick for him, the villains were in for an unpleasant surprise. Lathrop was the only man Harry knew whom he would have thought twice before meeting over drawn pistols or swords.

"That should hardly be a surprise to you," the countess pointed out. "You did serve with Lathrop on the Peninsula, after all. But then, I forgot. You make it a point to attend as little as possible to events going forth in the Society to which you were born. If you must know, it was reputed to be an arranged marriage. Lady Barrington, Lathrop's aunt, just happens to be the gel's godmother." His mama gave him an assessing glance. "You are not, I trust, planning to set up one of your flirtations with the gel, Harry? It is hardly in your style to involve yourself with women of gentility. If you are, however, I fear you will not find her in London. She is at Lathrop in the North Yorks for her lying in."

"And the other one?" queried Harry, who had no intention of satisfying his mama's curiosity. "You did say there were two married daughters?"

"Florence, Lady Moberly, the Marchioness of Leighton," supplied the countess. "A beauty of the first water with a reputation for being high in the instep. If *she* is your target, you will soon be made to catch cold, Harry."

Harry, however, was not attending. "Leighton," he repeated. "Of course. It would naturally make a deal more sense." Abruptly, he sprang to his feet. "It would seem that I am in your debt, Mother. You might even be pleased to know that the information you have just given me may in the end prove to be my undoing. I daresay that I was never in greater peril on the Continent than I am at this very moment, faced with the prospect of renewing my acquaintance with a veritable imp of a girl, who, besides thinking nothing of embroiling me in whatever harebrained toil she has got herself in, is not averse to beguiling me with her assurances that, not only is she unfavorably inclined toward marriage, but she has nothing to recommend her to a gentleman's attention. That, from a female who not only possesses the face and form of an Incomparable, but rides to the hounds with the fearlessness of an avenging angel."

"Good God, Harry." Scandalized, the countess bolted to her feet. "She is a marchioness. Think what you are doing."

"You may be sure that I have thought, until I have come to the conclusion that it is utterly useless to weigh the consequences." Bending down, he kissed his mama soundly on the cheek. "I'm afraid I am caught, Mama, not by the marchioness, who I doubt not is a diamond of the first water, but by Lady Francine, her unmarried younger sister."

Bidding his mama farewell, Harry had made his escape before the astonished countess could question him further. It was on the drive back to London, made in record time, that he saw his course laid out clearly before him. He found it amusing and not a little ironic that he had been ensnared at last by an innocent miss fresh from the country. What Lady Catherine, the green-eyed temptress, could not accomplish with all her sophisticated wiles, Lady Francie Powell had done all in a single moment.

No doubt, he mused, turning away from the window overlooking Grosvenor Square, it had been irrevocable from the moment fate had intervened to bring the damnably enchanting Miss Powell careening into his arms. If nothing else, the past two weeks had amply demonstrated that, no matter what might come of it, he could no more banish her from his thoughts than he could leave her to an uncertain fate at the hands of would-be murderers. Certainly, he was far too experienced in the ways of the world not to know what he was inviting by deliberately seeking her out in her sister's house—and, still, he had come.

Word of it would spread through every drawing room and ballroom, along with a deal of unwelcome speculation. Ransome had broken his ironclad rule for an innocent straight out of the schoolroom. His name would be entered in the betting books as an odds on favorite to wed Lady Francine Powell. Worse, having succumbed once to the wiles of a gently born female, he would be fair game for all the others. No doubt he would be forced to marry Miss Powell out of sheer self-preservation.

At least, he reflected in sardonic amusement, a man legshackled to Lady Francie was unlikely to suffer a surfeit of boredom. Indeed, he doubted not he would look back on his bachelorhood as a halcyon time marked by untroubled waters.

It was at that point that his attention was caught by the light tattoo of hurried footsteps beyond the drawing room door.

Conscious of a sudden sense of anticipation that was as acute as it was unprecedented, the earl turned as the doors were flung open—and was met with the unnerving sight of Lady Francine Elizabeth Powell appareled in the manner of a runaway bride in a white muslin pelisse over a white muslin round gown, white kid gloves, and a white gypsy hat, tied beneath the chin with a white ribbon and heavily draped in a concealing white gossamer veil of exquisite Venetian lace.

"My Lord Ransome," she exclaimed somewhat breathlessly and, smiling brightly through the veil, extended her hand in greeting. "And just in the nick of time, too. Leighton is only just leaving. I daresay if we hurry, we can still catch him before he is irretrievably lost to us."

"An end no doubt to be devoutly desired," observed Harry, wondering into what he had stumbled. If it was an elopement, then Leighton would seem to be a most unlikely groom. The marquis, after all, was already in possession of a wife.

Suddenly, his eyes hardened to steely points as one particularly unpleasant explanation presented itself. He knew Leighton only casually and by his reputation, which, on the whole, would not have led him to believe the man capable of taking advantage of a young girl's innocence. Still, it was not so uncommon an occurrence as to rule out the possibility.

He gave Francie a searching glance. "On the other hand," he said, "are you quite certain you wish to pursue your present course? Perhaps, Lady Powell, it would be wise to reconsider. I might even go so far as to suggest that there is a happier solution to your dilemma."

"But there *is* no other solution," Francie did not hesitate to inform him in no little agitation. "It is, in fact, a matter of life and death, my lord." Grasping his hand in hers, she impelled him urgently toward the doorway. "I'm afraid I must insist we hurry. There simply isn't time for lengthy explanations."

"No, I daresay there is not," Harry conceded grimly, feeling a clamp close like a vise on his vitals. Things had gone too far indeed if she was contemplating putting a period to her existence. At least the marquis would be made to see the error of his ways, he vowed darkly. Taking Francie's arm, he conducted her outside to his waiting curricle.

"There, my lord," Francie exclaimed at the curb. She pointed to a phaeton drawn by a matched pair of greys in tandem, which was just then vanishing round a corner onto Upper Brook Street. "The devil, I daresay we shall never catch him now."

"Rest assured, Lady Powell," Harry said chillingly as he lifted her to the seat. "I have yet to see a team to match my bays. You may be certain there is not the villain alive who could escape me."

"You cannot know how comforting that is to hear, my lord," replied Francie, somewhat taken aback at what would seem an excessive rancor on the part of the earl toward the marquis. "I cannot but think, however, that to refer to his lordship as a villain is just a trifle harsh in the circumstances. It is hardly unusual, after all, for a man in Leighton's position to keep a mistress as well as a wife. It is, in fact, perfectly acceptable behavior so long as one is careful to observe a modicum of discretion."

Harry's lips thinned to a grim line at what he perceived was meant to be a lecture on the protocol of something she should by all rights know nothing about. By God, hanging was too good for the bloody marquis! "Brava, Lady Powell." Settling on the seat beside her, he took up the ribbons and whip in the manner of a man who foresees a stern business before him. "If that is what he told you, then I can little wonder that you find yourself in your present predicament. It is one thing to keep a mistress on the side, but quite another to ruin an innocent female under one's protection." At that, he nodded curtly to the groom, who, no doubt recognizing the grim face of a harbinger of fate when he saw it, stepped hastily back. The bays plunged forward under Harry's sure hands. "I can only wonder that neither of you thought to consider your sister's probable feelings in the matter."

Francie, forced to grasp the side of the curricle to keep from being thrown out by the suddenness of their forward flight, was rendered momentarily speechless at so unfair an accusation. "You may be sure, my lord," she gasped, when she had got her balance back, "that my sister's feelings are of paramount importance to me. Naturally, I have not told her anything concerning this matter. I daresay she does not even suspect what Leighton is about. Furthermore, the marquis may be many things, but you may acquit him of taking advantage of a female's innocence. *That,* you may be certain, was lost long ago."

Harry, intent on threading his way through the traffic while keeping his sights on the phaeton better than a block in front of him, was moved by that declaration nearly to drive them both to ruin. Turning his head to Francie, he let his hands drop, and the bays shot forward—nearly into the path of an oncoming wagon. Only his quick reflexes and undoubted skill at the ribbons kept them from an almost certain collision.

"I suggest, my lord," Francie said tartly, attempting in the wake of near disaster to set her hat straight again, "that you keep your eyes to the fore. Or perhaps you should let me have the reins. I am far too young to wish to meet an untimely demise in a carriage accident."

"Rest assured, Lady Powell, there is not the slightest chance you will die in an accident," predicted Harry unpleasantly. "Far from it, you will undoubtedly live to meet a violent death by strangulation. Which would be only what you deserve. Perhaps, ma'am, you would oblige me by telling me exactly why we are in pursuit of your brother-in-law."

"But I told you. Or at least," she quickly amended, "I thought you understood. My brother-in-law, the marquis, is the object of a villainous plot to put him out of the way, and all because he has had the dire misfortune to fall victim to the wiles of a siren."

"Ah, yes," Harry nodded, beginning at last to put the afternoon's events in their proper perspective, "your encounter with the two murderous villains outside the Pork Pie Inn that you mentioned earlier. I must presume in light of our present circumstances that you did not see fit to enlighten the marquis as to the gist of their conversation."

"Well, naturally," replied Francie, with the air of one stating the obvious. "I could hardly warn him of his peril without relating the details of a certain event I daresay would profit neither of us to have revealed, my lord."

"I was wondering if you were going to bring that particular up," confessed Harry, glancing down at her. With a measure of satisfaction he saw her hands tighten convulsively in her lap. It would seem his assault on those lovely lips had not failed entirely to make an impression. "Perhaps you overrate the significance of what happened," he offered, checking the bays as a barouche turned off the street in front of them. "It would appear, after all, highly unlikely the chastened squire will be inclined to talk about it to anyone. In which case, it should be a relatively simple matter to wrap the whole in clean linen."

"Oh, indeed, my lord," Francie acerbically retorted, marveling at such naiveté in one of the earl's reputation. "You could marry me, and that would solve everything. I do wish you will be serious, Ransome."

"You may be certain that I am prepared to treat the matter with all the seriousness that it deserves," said Harry, who, having come some time ago to the conclusion that marrying Lady Powell was indeed the most felicitous solution to any number of difficulties, not the least of which was his own happiness, could hardly have been less prone to view the matter lightly. "It does occur to me, however, that a deal of trouble might be averted were you simply to lay the whole before your brother-in-law. I daresay he is not an unreasonable man."

Francie shrugged. "In the norm, I should say he is exceedingly rational. Unfortunately, he is in the toils of an unruly passion for a female who, I have been reliably informed, would not hesitate to cut his stick for him. Trust me, my lord, in his present state, he is not to be depended upon to think in a rational manner."

Harry, in a similar case, could only sympathize with the marquis. "I begin to see your point, Lady Powell," he said, neatly feather-edging a blind corner. "You still have not, however, explained what you hope to accomplish by following Leighton."

"But it is obvious, is it not?" Francie declared. "I intend to discover for myself the whereabouts of the object of Leighton's obsession. Only when I have seen Madame Noire for myself shall I be able to determine the best manner in which to reveal her true character to my brother-in-law."

"Madame Noire?" echoed Harry, frowning. "By that, do you intend a purely figurative expression or is that the name by which you know her?"

"I believe it to be her name, since the villains called her by it. Why? Are you acquainted with her?"

"Only by reputation," confessed Harry, little wondering at Lady Powell's concern if Madame Veronique

Noire was the female with whom Leighton was dally-ing.

"I knew you would be of immeasurable help to me. Which is why your arrival was so fortuitous."

"No doubt I am gratified I was able to accommodate you," Harry said in exceedingly dry accents.

"I was sure you would be, my lord," Francie did not hesitate to inform him. "You cannot imagine the terrible quandary in which I found myself. For if you must know, my sister insists on keeping my activities confined to only those pursuits suitable to a young lady about to make her come-out."

"A hideous prospect," ventured his lordship.

"I knew you would understand," Francie replied feelingly. Indeed, he could not know what a relief it was to have someone at last with whom she could speak plainly. "Which is why I had come to despair of ever finding you again."

At that ingenuous pronouncement and its seeming implications, Harry shot a startled glance at her. "I begin to see your dilemma."

"But of course you do. After all, I was hardly likely to run into you at a tea party for young ladies, and you were the only one I could think of who would be in a position to help me. You must not think, how-ever, that I mean to jeopardize your position. I am perfectly aware that it would never do for you to be seen with me. Which is why I have chosen to remain incognito."

"How very foresighted of you," observed Harry, who had been aware for some time that they had been attracting a deal of notice from any number of passersby who knew him on sight. "However, I feel obligated to point out that your unique choice of costume is certain to arouse a deal of speculation."

"Yes, I was sure it would," agreed Francie, apparently pleased that he had so readily grasped the obvious. "That is precisely why I chose it. That, and because it was the only thing ready to hand with a veil. It is, nevertheless, utterly perfect. I daresay everyone will be trying to guess the identity of Ransome's newest *inamorata.*"

"Oh, you may be sure of it," said Harry, thinking rumor was more likely to have him married by morning. "It would seem, however, that our efforts may have been entirely wasted. The marquis's apparent destination, far from being a tryst with a Paphian, is undoubtedly his private club."

Francie, brought to the realization that Ransome was pulling up with every intention of abandoning the chase, was moved to an immediate protest. "But surely you cannot mean to leave off here? You cannot possibly be certain this is where he means to stop."

"No, but you may be certain it is where *I* mean to call a halt. You have an exceedingly odd notion of my character if you believe I should think nothing of parading a female down the length of St. James's Street. I daresay you would find little to recommend in being ogled by town beaus from every window."

Francie, observing with no little dismay the marquis's carriage disappearing down the one street which was by unwritten rule banned to women of gentle extraction, declared incredulously of Ransome. "But what can it possibly matter—if no one knows who I am?"

"You are mistaken, surely," Harry replied, proceeding on Piccadilly past St. James's Street. "*I* know who you are, and that is sufficient."

"*Oh!*" exclaimed Francie. Arms folded, she flounced back in her seat. "I might have known. Another of those insurmountable barriers for the benefit of keeping women in their places. How I detest them. And you, my lord. I thought you, of all people, would be above allowing yourself to be bound by them."

Harry, who knew, if she did not, how little it profited one to openly flaunt the conventions, could not but be aware he had slipped considerably in Lady Powell's estimation. Clearly, the course he had set for himself was not to be a smooth one. Indeed, he doubted not it was to be fraught with any number of harrowing pitfalls through which somehow he must safely conduct the headstrong young innocent without seeming to play the part of protector. Nor was that all or the worst of the difficulties he saw before him.

Lady Powell, he could not but be aware, had thus far demonstrated a remarkable insouciance toward him, which he found more than a little daunting, not to mention injurious to his self-esteem. It was readily apparent that, while she was perfectly willing to avail herself of his services in a tight, she would seem to demonstrate a total disregard for his various manly attributes.

Harry, who had long been considered a Catch of

the Marriage Mart, had never been one to fool himself into thinking it was not his fortune and title that made him so desirable a candidate. While, therefore, he could not but find Lady Powell's indifference less than complimentary, he was moved to a sardonic appreciation of the fact that she clearly had designs neither on himself nor his worldly possessions. Had she deliberately set out to ensnare him, she could have found no better way to capture his interest, never mind that he strongly suspected the reason for her state of mind had less to do with him than with the fact that, believing herself without any feminine accomplishments, she utterly failed to consider herself as a candidate for his serious intentions.

"I beg your pardon, Lady Powell, if I have failed to live up to your expectations," he said with only a hint of dryness. "On the other hand, it did occur to me that calling attention to our pursuit would accomplish very little. Very likely it would lead only to your own unveiling with all the unenviable repercussions that must bring. In which case, at risk of seeming impertinent, perhaps I might offer a suggestion."

"I wish you will not be absurd, my lord," replied Francie, who was already regretting her impetuous outburst. Indeed, she had suffered an inexplicably hollow sensation at the thought that his lordship might see fit to immediately sever any further connections. But then, she could hardly feel otherwise, she told herself firmly. Naturally, she could not wish to lose her one and only contact with the broader world. "Far from viewing it as an impertinence," she added magnanimously, "I should naturally be grateful for any ideas you might have."

Harry, who had little difficulty guessing her probable train of thought, suppressed a smile of sardonic amusement. "Then perhaps I should begin by telling you that Madame Veronique Moire is an actress, who is noted for her various brief alliances with men of rank and influence."

"An actress!" exclaimed Francie, with a swift leap of interest. "No wonder Leighton was so easily duped. I daresay Madame Noire is adept at pulling the wool over any number of men's eyes."

"Exactly so," Harry agreed. "Which is why it occurs to me that *I* should be the one to seek the woman out. No one would be any the wiser. Naturally, I should report to you everything that I am able to learn about her and her intentions toward your brother-in-law. After which, we shall no doubt be in a better position to determine what may be done to extricate him from his entanglement."

"It is kind of you to offer, my lord," Francie replied doubtfully, it suddenly having occurred to *her* that she did not quite like the notion of exposing Ransome to the wiles of the seductress. "I daresay, however, it is unfair to ask you to undertake such a mission for someone whom, after all, you do not even know."

"No doubt I am gratified at your concern, Lady Powell. However, I do not foresee that I shall incur any undue risks. I, you will admit, am free to go where I choose without censure. Nor would it be unduly remarked were I to call on a female of Madame

Noire's dubious reputation. It would, in fact, be only what is expected of me. Besides, it shall no doubt appeal to my adventurous nature."

"I suppose I cannot find fault with your arguments," Francie admitted grudgingly after giving the matter her serious consideration. "Still, how detestable it is that I shall be required to attend ladies' tea parties while you have all the fun."

"You have my sincerest sympathies, Lady Powell," Harry assured her with only the faintest twitch at the corners of his lips. "And now, perhaps it would be wise to return you to your sister's house without further delay. It occurs to me the marchioness will be wondering where you have gone."

"The devil," exclaimed Francie. "I was in such a hurry, I did not take time to think what I should tell her. Especially when she catches me in the clothes she wore to Patrick's christening. I daresay she will think it exceedingly strange."

"No doubt something will come to you," Harry predicted dryly, having come about on a direct course back to Grosvenor Square. "In the meantime, it occurs to me that I should like to have you promise you will not take matters into your own hands before I have the opportunity to report back to you. There would seem to be little sense, after all, in alerting our quarry to the fact that we are on to her."

"No, I suppose that would not be to our advantage," agreed Francie with no little reluctance. "On the other hand, something may arise when you are nowhere at hand. I daresay you would not expect me to sit idly by while opportunity slips through my fingers. In all fairness, my lord, I feel I should not promise more than I can keep."

"I see your point," said Harry, who did not doubt that, should such an incident present itself, Lady Powell would indeed find herself hard put to resist temptation.

"But of course you do," Francie replied confidently. "You are, after all, a man of action, a soldier, who recognizes that contingencies all too often crop up when they are least expected. No, I fear the best I can offer is my word that I shall do nothing in this matter, save in the event I am presented with a fortuitous opportunity too important to let pass. In which case, I shall make every effort to leave word for you as to my purpose and destination."

Harry, well aware that such a promise left a great deal to be desired, had little recourse but to comfort himself with the knowledge that he was not likely to be offered anything better.

"Agreed, Lady Powell," he said. Pulling up before her sister's mansion, he solemnly offered Francie his hand to seal the contract. "It shall be our secret pact, known only to us."

Francie, placing her palm in his, experienced a sudden, unwitting thrill at the feel of slender, masculine fingers closing firmly over hers. Even through the glove he wore, she could not but be acutely aware of the strength in that hand, and the gentleness that enabled him to wield the reins with a feathery light touch. She did not have to see it to know that the palm, while limber, was callused, as befitted a man noted for his outdoor pursuits. It was, in fact, she doubted not, just the sort of hand—strong, shapely, and supple—that she most admired in a man.

Unreasonably, she blushed at the thought.

Indeed, she could only be grateful for the concealing fabric of the veil, as it came to her suddenly that she had allowed her own small, eminently capable member to reside in the earl's larger one far longer than was strictly acceptable.

"Well, then," she blurted, pulling free with an equally unseemly haste. "I shall look forward to hearing from you, my lord. No. No need to leave your horses. I am perfectly capable of getting down without assistance."

Gathering up her skirts, she climbed nimbly down to the street, to stand for a moment looking up at him. "I must thank you, my lord, not only for your timely assistance, but for an enjoyable outing. You may be sure I shall look forward to seeing you again—to hear what you have learned, naturally."

"Naturally, Lady Powell," Harry replied, lifting his hat to her. *"Au revoir* for now."

Francie, waiting only long enough for him to set the cattle in motion, turned and fled into the house.

Six

Fortunately Reynolds, it seemed, was occupied elsewhere in the house. As Florence, too, was nowhere in sight, Francie was able to slip upstairs and change into a pastel pink sarcenet walking dress in time for her five o'clock outing with Miss Wilmington of the Sussex Wilmingtons with no one the wiser.

She had, in fact, only just finished concealing Florence's borrowed white christening costume when Florence, looking pale but composed, made her appearance at Francie's door.

"Francie," she said, poking her head in, "I hope you will forgive this intrusion. There is something I wish to discuss with you. May I come in?"

Francie crossed immediately to take Flo's hands in hers. "Pray forgive my stupid tongue. One day I shall learn to keep it between my teeth. I swear I never meant to hurt your feelings."

"Please do not swear, Francie, and, no, of course you did not mean to hurt me." Something in Florence's aspect relaxed ever so slightly. "Any more than I meant to snap off your nose. Now let us forget the whole unhappy incident. As it happens, I have just received your vouchers for Almack's. To celebrate, I thought we should go to the theatre tonight."

"But I should like that above all things," Francie declared, trying not to analyze why she should have felt a flurry of excitement at the prospect. It could not be because the theatre was one place she might encounter a certain gimlet-eyed nobleman. Indeed, such a thought was patently absurd, she told herself. No doubt it was only because she had never had recourse before to see a play performed by a professional troupe of actors in a real theatre.

Flo smiled, apparently as relieved as Francie to have the sisterly spat behind her. "Good," she said, giving Francie's hands a small squeeze before releasing them. "There is, of course, the dinner at Lady Bellows's. I daresay if you have Miss Wilmington return you home no later than six-thirty, you will have plenty of time to change. And, Francie," she added, pausing at the door, "I trust you are ready to be launched into what will be an uninterrupted schedule of events. From now on there will be no more tea parties, only galas, balls, and impromptu routs."

"You may be sure I am ready for anything that will deliver me from young ladies' tea parties," Francie averred with a comical grimace. "Even if it does mean I shall be relegated to the sidelines with the rest of the wallflowers."

That, however, was not to be the case. In the days following her momentous drive with Ransome, Francie was to discover that Florence could not have been more accurate in her prediction that there would be little time in future for boredom, or private reflections, for that matter. The Season had begun in earnest, which meant there might be as many as three or four balls on practically any given night, not to mention any number of other entertainments for which Florence received invitations.

While Florence Anne Marie Powell may have been denied the success to which she had looked as the acknowledged Beauty of the family, the Marchioness of Leighton was a different proposition altogether. She, by virtue of her name and rank alone, commanded no little influence among the fashionables of London. Nor was she averse to wielding it.

No sooner had Florence let it officially be known that she was sponsoring her younger sister's come-out, than the house on Grosvenor Square was inundated with invitations. Nor was Francie left to dawdle, unnoticed, at the whirl of social events that she attended. Far from it.

Francie, greatly to her surprise, discovered that she was much sought after by males and females alike of the younger set, a circumstance that she did not hesitate to attribute to Florence's influence. The truth was, however, that her youthful exuberance, coupled as it was with a wholly unaffected manner, served to make Francie the center of attraction wherever she went. The young ladies liked her for her frank speech and unassuming air of sociability, while the young gentlemen found much to recommend in a beauty who was not only able to discuss practically any aspect of horsemanship, including the training and breeding of prime bits of blood, but actually seemed to enjoy such masculine topics of conversation.

In short, while she had yet to attract the notice of the older, more case-hardened Men About Town, she was well on her way to attaining a more than modest success. Certainly, Florence could not have been more pleased with her sister's progress, a circumstance that had only a little to do with the fact that Francie's success must inevitably redound to Florence's credit. Flo seemed sincerely pleased for Francie's sake. As for Francie herself, she could not but be aware that she was enjoying herself a deal more than she could possibly have anticipated.

Still, if either sister had been perfectly honest with the other, they must each have admitted to a fly in the ointment. Leighton remained least seen in his wife's affairs, and Ransome had yet to make any attempt to communicate with Francie.

In the days following her secret pact with Ransome, Francie was kept too busy to chafe at having been relegated to the role of a silent co-conspirator left, for all practical purposes, in the dark. Still, she could not stop herself from looking at every ball, fete, and gala she attended for a tall masculine figure with carelessly combed hair of a dark golden-brown and eyes the piercing blue of rapiers. And how not, she reflected one afternoon, flinging herself across her bed, when, though his handsome person was conspicuous by its absence, his name was constantly on everyone's lips!

And, indeed, it seemed the whole world had nothing better to do than to speculate as to the identity of the Earl of Ransome's newest *inamorata*. Lady Fitzhugh reported having seen the earl shamelessly parading the female in question through the City streets in his curricle in broad daylight, a testimony vouchsafed to by more than a dozen other witnesses. The consensus of opinion, that the mysterious beauty, unlike Ransome's previous love birds, was a woman of gentility, a nobleman's wife, being the most popular theory, was based on a single damning piece of evidence: Ransome, a noted connoisseur of beautiful women, would hardly have spread his mantle of protection over an antidote, which left no other viable explanation for why the lady should have chosen to conceal her face behind a veil. The other, more glaring singularity, her appearance all in pristine white, while leading some in the absence of a notice in the *Gazette* of Ransome's recent nuptials to deduce she was newly arrived from the East Indies and others to insist that she was clearly a feminist sympathizer endowed with a keen sense of irony, had given rise to the appellate that was on everyone's lips.

She was the White Rose, and she was the most intriguing topic of conversation to hit the fashionable circles since Lady Fenway had run away with her groom.

Francie, forced to listen with her tongue between her teeth, at first derived no little entertainment from finding herself the object of so much speculation. When, however, nearly a week had passed without a word from Ransome, she could not but realize the subject had begun to pall on her. There was, after all, little to amuse in the thought that Ransome had very probably taken exception to all the furor in which his name figured not insignificantly. It came to her that, disenchanted with the entire affair, he had likely forgotten all about his archplotter and, taking himself off to the country, was determined to rusticate until the storm should finally blow over.

One greater possibility, even less appealing than the first—that, having tracked down his quarry, he had found Madame Noire as utterly irresistible as she was reputed to be—was simply not to be thought of. And yet, Francie did think of it, and with annoying frequency, most often whenever she was just on the point of falling asleep after having arrived home in the wee hours of the morning.

Drat, thought Francie, consigning the earl without remorse to the devil. At the very least he might have had the decency to keep to the letter of their bargain. He *could* have made an effort to see her one last time.

It was, consequently, with something less than an overwhelming sense of eagerness that Francie looked forward that night to her first appearance at Almack's Assembly Rooms. Certainly, that most elite of Marriage Marts would be the *last* place to be graced by the notorious Earl of Ransome.

The evening at Almack's began well enough. Though Francie had yet to be approved for the waltz, she was kept well occupied in the various country dances or chitchatting with any number of new acquaintances. As the hour of eleven approached, however, when the doors would be irrevocably barred to any latecomers, no matter who they might happen to be, Francie sat alone, waiting for the supper dance to begin.

She was just comforting herself with the thought that Miss Wilmington and Miss Chalmers had promised to join her as soon as the waltz set was ended, when she became aware of a sudden stir, followed by a hush over the ballroom. She looked curiously up— and was met with the stunning sight of a tall elegant figure entering to the accompanying chime of the clock striking eleven.

Ransome! Good God, it could not be. And yet there was no mistaking the broad, muscular shoulders, admirably encased in a black double-breasted cutaway, or the long, tapering torso, shown to remarkable advantage in a white marcella waistcoat. She doubted there was another man alive who could wear black knee-breeches, white clock-work stockings, and black patent slippers with diamond buckles with such careless ease.

The devil, she thought, acutely aware that a slow flush was sweeping from her lowest extremities upward to at last reach her cheeks. He had come. But, why, of all places, should he have chosen Almack's to make his appearance!

That he was there at all was enough to set tongues wagging for a month. If he deigned further to approach a nobody who had only just made her curtsey in Society, he would create a stir on the order of an incident of major proportions. Certainly, there was not a soul in attendance who was not wondering at that very moment what, or, more pertinently, who was the object of Ransome's slow saunter down the one hundred feet that comprised the length of the ballroom.

Francie, who only a few hours before had been wishing above all things to run into the maddeningly elusive nobleman, was now fervently desirous of having the dance floor open up and swallow her. Hastily she lowered her eyes while attempting to assume an aspect of indifference, only to peep up again through the veil of her eyelashes to check the earl's forward progress.

She experienced a measure of relief that was to be exceedingly short-lived at sight of Ransome in close conversation with Sally Jersey, one of the patronesses. The sudden, agitated flutter of Sally Jersey's black lace folding fan, not to mention the lady's startled glance in Francie's direction, left little doubt who was the subject of their conversation.

In another moment, everyone in the ballroom was aware of it.

Francie, studiously watching the couples move about the dance floor, could almost feel the crackle of interest as Ransome, with Sally Jersey on his arm, came to stand before her chair.

"Lady Francine," said Sally Jersey, her lively eyes keen with speculation, "his lordship, the Earl of Ransome, has requested that you be allowed to stand up with him for the waltz. I have given my approval on the grounds that I feel you are a well-bred young woman with unexceptional manners. And because Ransome has assured me that His Grace, the Duke of Lathrop, requested that he make himself known to you."

"My brother-in-law has spoken often of his lordship," Francie answered, dipping a curtsey. "You are very kind, ma'am, to introduce us."

"Nonsense. I am deriving no little entertainment from the sensation the two of you are creating. Enjoy yourself, my dear," she added, blithely waving her closed fan over her shoulder as she made her departure. "I daresay you have just embarked on a whole new career."

"She is right, you know," Francie whispered fiercely, as she placed her hand in Ransome's and allowed herself to be led out onto the dance floor. "Could you not have picked a less conspicuous place to contact me? I hope you realize I shall now become the rage overnight, and all because of you. Worse, it will undoubtedly be all over Town by tomorrow morning that you and I are—are . . . I mean that you have . . ."

"Singled you out for my attentions?" Harry finished for her. "Is the notion so very distasteful to you, Lady Powell?" he queried mildly, as, her hand in his, he swung her around to face him.

Francie's heart leaped as she felt his firm arm slip lightly around her waist. Indeed, she had the most peculiar sensation of having just run a foot race as she felt her pulse, not to mention her respiration, rapidly accelerating beyond the normal rate. Worse, she seemed to have lost the ability to think with any coherence.

"Distasteful, my lord?" she echoed, staring up at

him with a curiously startled expression. "No, of course not," she added then, seeming to shake herself out of her abstraction. "Naturally I should be flattered, if I did not know how patently absurd it would be to consider such a thing even for a moment. I am not so green as to suppose you could ever form an interest in me. You are here, are you not, because you have something to tell me about Madame Noire?"

A smile, faintly ironic, touched Harry's lips. Only the inimitable Lady Powell could possibly have mistaken his purpose in deliberately seeking her out at Almack's Assembly Rooms. And only Lady Powell would see the inevitable outcome of his singular attentions in the light of an annoyance.

He had made her a *success fou* overnight. Anyone would have thought from Lady Powell's reaction that he had condemned her to the penal colonies.

"As a matter of fact," Harry said, swinging Francie into the gliding steps of the waltz, "I have found out a great deal about Madame Noire. The lady, a full-blown beauty, presently occupies a modest house on Swallow Street, which Leighton visits on a regular basis. While her accomplishments on stage are only minimal at best, she enjoys a certain popularity as a private entertainer. She has a passion for gambling, which she enjoys playing for high stakes. For this purpose, she is known to frequent a private gaming house known as the Goldfinch."

Francie screwed her face into a comical frown. "The Goldfinch. I should think that was an odd name for a gaming establishment."

"I believe I should not be mistaken in saying it was

named after a Portuguese singer, whose voice has
been compared, somewhat whimsically perhaps, to
that of a songbird," Harry confided with an humble
air. "I have been intimately acquainted with the
owner of the establishment for any number of years."

"Oh, but that is marvelous!" Francie exclaimed,
her face instantly brightening.

"No doubt I am gratified at your approval," returned Harry, suffering a sudden, inexplicable qualm
at the effusiveness of her response.

"I had been wondering how I should gain admission," Francie did not hesitate to inform him. "If you
are on intimate terms with the owner, that, however,
is hardly a problem."

"Yes, I see what you mean," replied Harry, who
could not but think such a conclusion must depend
on one's relative point of view. Naturally, he relished
the notion of introducing an innocent female of refinement into the unsavory environs of his own private
gambling house—a female, moreover, who had the
distinction of being related to a duke, a marquis, and
an earl. Good God, if he did not find himself facing
Lathrop across a dueling field, he could look forward
to a meeting with Leighton and at the very least the
prospect of a tongue-lashing from the irate earl whom
he had every intention of making his papa-in-law. "On
the other hand, I wonder if you have thought the matter through. Perhaps it has not occurred to you that
an adventure of this nature entails far greater risk than
did your surrender to irresistible impulse in the
Quorn country. This time you can hardly claim the
distinction of being a nobody. I should even go so far

as to say you will most certainly be recognized should
you put in an appearance at the Goldfinch."

Francie, far from being discouraged at so obvious
a drawback to her burgeoning plan, and in spite of
an unwonted tendency to lose her train of thought
in the face of any number of other distractions—not
the least of which were an acute awareness of being
clasped in the circle of the earl's strong, muscular
arm, a spellbinding sense of Ransome's masculinely
athletic grace, not to mention the sublime feeling
that she was floating on air and a disconcerting wish
that the waltz might go on forever—was instead ready
with an immediate reply. "Really, my lord, you disappoint me," she said dreamily, her head tilted to one
side as Ransome whirled her around to the dance
steps. "I should have thought the solution was obvious. Naturally, I shall not go as Lady Francine Elizabeth Powell. I shall make my appearance at the
Goldfinch as your newest *inamorata,* the White Rose."

"Ah. Now why, I wonder, did I not think of that?"
marveled Harry, who had spent the past several days
fending off the importunate queries of his intimates
as to the identity of the mysterious vision in white. "Of
course that must answer to everything, save, perhaps
how you intend to absent yourself from your sister's
watchful presence," he added, noting an exceedingly
attractive young woman who, since she was eyeing
them from the row of matrons with something less
than her wholehearted approval, he judged to be the
marchioness. "I trust I shall not be required to escort
Leighton's wife to the Goldfinch in order to meet his
mistress."

He was rewarded for that bit of absurdity with a gurgling laugh from Francie along with a roguish look that quite took his breath away. "In the circumstances, my lord, I believe it would be better if on the night in question, I plead a headache and retire early to bed. Let us say tomorrow night at nine, since Flo is promised to Lady Trowbridge's, who happens to be a dear friend of my mother's, which means Flo would not dream of crying off. I shall have little difficulty slipping out by the back way, where you will of course be waiting for me."

"Oh, indubitably," agreed Harry with the air of one who was accustomed to participating in any number of schemes designed to ruin an innocent female's reputation, not to mention devastate what was left of his own already tarnished name. "It will naturally appeal to my adventurous nature."

As there seemed little point in bringing up any further objections, such as the distinct possibility of encountering her brother-in-law in the company of Madame Noire, the conceivable chance of having her disguise penetrated by someone discerning enough to recognize her voice or mannerisms, the unlooked for circumstance of her sister's returning home early to find the chick had flown the coop, or any of a dozen other potentialities for mischance that readily occurred to him, Harry lapsed into silence, contenting himself with enjoying what might in the end prove his one and only dance with Lady Powell. It would hardly have done, after all, to refuse to take part in what he privately viewed as a recipe for disaster. An astute judge of character, he had long since deduced that the irrepressible Lady Francie would not hesitate to attempt the thing on her own.

Francie, who was naturally light of foot and had, at Lucy's insistence, been carefully tutored in the waltz by no less a personage than the Duke of Lathrop himself, was too preoccupied with other, far more pertinent things to notice the sudden halt in conversation. It had never occurred to her before that dancing in a man's arms could be so wonderfully blissful as waking up in the morning to the first snowfall of winter, or so pleasurable as gliding across a frozen pond on ice skates beneath a cloud-dappled sky, or so marvelously sweet as witnessing the first wobbly steps of a new foal or. . . . Here, her imagination failed her.

She could no more come up with the words to describe the feelings she was experiencing than she could explain why Ransome should have been the one to generate them.

It was enough that the world seemed to have magically withdrawn somehow, leaving her and Ransome swirling to the music in a universe all their own—until the strains of the waltz came suddenly and inevitably to an end. It was only then, when she had been flung rudely back to earth, that she was struck by a startling thought.

When she was with Ransome, she did not mind at all that she was a female. Indeed, for the first time in her life, it came to her that there might be a deal to recommend in being just what she was.

It was an astounding realization, one that led inevitably to a host of disturbing feelings, not the least of which was the dizzying sensation of being poised on the brink of a precipice.

It was then, when she was trying to grapple with what seemed to loom just beyond her comprehension, that Ransome's voice, sharp-edged with concern, impinged at last upon her consciousness.

"Lady Powell? Lady Francie, are you feeling all right?"

"What?" Francie, still in the grip of sublime revelation, became suddenly aware of the fact that she must have been staring like a mindless idiot for several seconds into Ransome's ruggedly handsome features. To her further horror, she felt at her rude awakening an immediate hot rush of blood to her cheeks. "Yes, yes. I am fine," she asserted in a mortifyingly breathless voice, and, like the most detestable of simpering females, had immediate recourse to her fan. "It is only that it is a trifle close in here, do you not think?"

"Practically unbearable," Harry assured her with what she would surely have perceived to be a glint of amusement in the heavy-lidded eyes had she not been studiously looking anywhere but at him. Indeed, she could not but be grateful when, having reached her chair near the entrance to the supper room, she was immediately besieged by a group of young bloods eager for the honor of her company.

"Lady Powell," murmured Ransome, bending briefly over her hand. "It has been a pleasure."

"My lord," Francie found the wit to reply. Then he was gone, weaving his way through the crowd toward the exit.

It really was too absurd, thought Francie, who was

left to decide who among her bevy of new admirers should lead her into the supper dance. How preposterous that a single dance with the Earl of Ransome should suddenly have made her so instantly fashionable! She was the same Francie Powell, who only minutes before had been left to sit by herself while waiting for the waltz set to end. Or was she? she wondered, acutely aware that her pulse had yet to resume its normal pace.

She was given little time to analyze that particular question during the rest of her evening at Almack's. When she was not dancing, a circumstance that occurred only between sets, she was kept far too busy making certain no single one of her clamoring admirers was made to feel he was esteemed over any of the others.

This, she discovered, was no easy task. The merest glance of her eyes—which, she was informed by one ardent gentleman who was, she judged, old enough to know better, were dazzling gems—was viewed as a sign of her favor. The request of a glass of punch was enough to render the fortunate bearer an object of envy, while an inadvertent smile might be sufficient to incite an argument.

It was all very trying to Francie, who had never been given to the practice of diplomacy. She was, in fact, on the point of wishing them all to the devil, when she was rescued by Florence's announcement that, due to another engagement, it was time they were going.

"Thank heavens," exclaimed Francie, as soon as they were safely tucked away in the carriage. "Did you ever see anything like it? Clearly, the whole world is mad. I believe I shall not soon forgive Ransome for turning me over to the wolves."

"Ransome?" Florence echoed, turning to eye her sister strangely. "You say his name as easily as if you had known him all your life. Indeed, I had the oddest impression that you were not entirely strangers to one another."

"No doubt that is because we are not, really," Francie replied, mentally kicking herself for allowing her guard to relax. Flo, after all, was anything but a slowtop. "Phillip has told me ever so much about his lordship that I feel as if we are intimately acquainted. Do you remember when Phillip related the tale of how Ransome saved his life? I thought then that Ransome must be the bravest man alive—next to Phillip, of course." Francie, artlessly stifling a yawn behind her gloved hand, glanced sideways at Florence. "It was kind of his lordship to come tonight, was it not? Naturally, it was all because of Phillip, but, really, I wish that he had not. I am afraid being a *success fou* is not all that it is cracked up to be. I daresay I shall discover it was a deal easier being a mere nobody."

Florence, who had been unusually quiet for the past several minutes, turned sharply on Francie at that guileless observation. "Faith, Francie, only you would come up with something so ridiculous. Have you any notion of the magnitude of his lordship's condescension in making an appearance at the Assembly Rooms, let alone having as his sole purpose paying you the distinction of his notice? I daresay there is not a soul who will believe he was motivated by a sense of friendship to your brother-in-law let alone by anything remotely resembling kindness. I cannot bring *myself* to believe it. The Earl of Ransome is not known for his generosity or his altruism, but for something altogether different."

"His lordship, you mean, is a rake," pronounced Francie baldly.

"Yes, if you must be so blunt," Florence returned shortly. "He is also a man of influence, though he seldom chooses to wield it. His father, the former earl, was a noted Corinthian and an arbiter of fashion, and his mama, the countess, was one of the most celebrated hostesses in London, until she chose to retire to Brighton. In spite of Ransome's predilection for a different class of women and though he must be considered dangerous, he has never ceased to be regarded as a prime catch of the Marriage Mart. Nor can one disregard the fact that he has yet to set up his nursery. I daresay there can be only one interpretation for tonight's singular event, Francie, and while I should never approve of such a match for you, we may count ourselves fortunate that he has inexplicably taken an interest in you."

Francie stared in stunned dismay at her sister. "But that is not at all the case," she declared, perhaps more forcefully than she had intended. "Ransome is not the least interested in me, and I am in no danger of receiving an offer from him. If I were, however, I should feel deeply honored. You are very much mistaken in his character if you cannot see that he is a man of rare integrity and honor."

"No doubt you are in the right of it, Francie,"

Florence said, striving for a reasonable tone in the face of her sister's unexpectedly impassioned outburst. "Indeed, I can only hope for your sake that you are. On the other hand, it little signifies. The truth is he is a man with a questionable reputation, who might ruin you just as easily as he has made you a success. He has, after all, chosen deliberately to set himself apart from the world to which he rightfully belongs, and that cannot reflect well on him or his intentions."

"Oh, pooh!" was Francie's telling comment on that piece of absurdity. "I daresay there might be any number of reasons why he should have given up Society, not the least of which is that it must seem dreadfully trivial to spend one's time going to dinners and galas when one has been used to risking one's life for king and country. If he is dangerous, it is only to those who deserve to be taken down a peg. And if he cared for me enough to offer, you may be sure I should be proud to be his wife, no matter what the world might think of him—or me, for that matter."

This glowing encomium, far from relieving her sister's mind where Ransome and his possible motives were concerned, clearly had the opposite effect. "Francie, good heavens!" exclaimed Flo in no little consternation. "If I did not know better, I should say you are in love with the man."

"Perhaps I am, a little," Francie retorted, in no mood to be conciliatory. "I daresay it would be marvelous if I did *not* love him for saving Phillip's life. I am not such an idiot, however, as to fool myself into believing he could ever care for me, save, perhaps, in the light of a troublesome younger sister. So let us please say no more on the subject of the Earl of Ransome."

Florence, for once in her life, did not push the subject, but it could hardly have been said that she was made in the least easier by Francie's frank outburst. On the contrary, having herself a measure of experience in the vagaries of love, she was very much afraid that Francie displayed all the symptoms of one who simply had yet to know her own heart.

But that was ridiculous, Flo told herself. After all, Francie, for all her impulsiveness, was possessed of an essentially practical nature. She had only just met the earl for a very few moments. She simply could not have fallen so completely for him in so short a time. And yet, Florence could not escape the notion that her sister would bear watching. It would never do, after all, for Francie to make the error of setting her sights on a man like Ransome. She knew only too well that it could only end in disappointment, and that was one heartache from which Florence was determined to do all in her power to preserve her sister. She would not let Francie make the same mistakes that she had.

Francie, had Florence only known it, was following a similar line of reasoning. Hardly had Florence pointed out that Francie gave every impression of one in love than the truth had struck Francie full force. She would not go so far as to admit she had lost her heart to the earl, but she could hardly deny what she had felt in his arms. Obviously, the peculiar sensations she had experienced were of a singular nature, which could only be attributed to an irresistible attraction to Ransome, and that would never do, she told herself. Indeed, it promised fair to ruin everything.

In light of recent events, she could hardly expect to maintain her objectivity if every time she was in Ransome's presence she were to be constantly prey to sensations of a similar discommoding nature. Really, it was too bad of him to place her in such an untenable position, she thought irritably. Not, of course, that he could help being an irresistible force. Indeed, she doubted not that there were any number of females who had fallen victim to that same devastating influence. Handsome, athletic, possessed of a generous nature and a powerful intellect, not to mention a strong propensity for adventure, Ransome, after all, was her ideal of what a man should be.

Upon sober reflection, it seemed almost a forgone conclusion that, if she had not done so already, she most certainly was fated to fall head over ears in love with the irresistible Earl of Ransome. Unfortunately, the same could hardly be said of him. A man noted for the beautiful women he kept, after all, could hardly be expected to form a *tendre* for Francine Powell, she reminded herself, and she had a particular aversion to the notion of making a cake of herself over a man who could not possibly feel anything more for her than a generous impulse to be of service to the sister-in-law of his closest friend. In light of Ransome's kindness, the last thing she could wish was to embarrass him by letting him see that she had fallen victim to a hopeless passion.

She supposed she could at least be grateful to Flo

ZEBRA HOME SUBSCRIPTION SERVICE, INC.

120 BRIGHTON ROAD

P.O. BOX 5214

CLIFTON, NEW JERSEY 07015-5214

lll..l..l.lll....ll.l.l..l.ll.l..l.ll..ll..ll..l

for one thing, she decided. Now that she had been made aware of the danger, she would make certain in future never to betray herself or her unfortunate feelings to his lordship. Indeed, she would rather die than let him see that she was falling in love with him. No doubt she would eventually get over her affliction. In a decade or two, she would be able to look back on her one and only affair of the heart with little more than a pang of regret.

In the meantime, she thought in a practical vein, there was little use in fretting over what could not be helped. If she was doomed to an unrequited love, then she might as well make the most of her short time with Ransome.

Her decision made, she should have experienced a measure of comfort, but, strangely, she felt only a ridiculous urge to succumb to a fit of the vapors.

Consequently, she could only be relieved when Flo, complaining of a headache, suggested they forego Lady Winslow's gala to which they were promised and instead go home. Francie had a great deal to think about, not the least of which was what she was going to wear on the following night for her assignation with Ransome.

Seven

"Bless me, m'lady. Her ladyship will have our heads for this," declared Daisy, standing back to gaze in wide-eyed dismay at her mistress. "Are you sure you know what you're doing? You're taking an awful gamble, wearing that gown. Even if I can put it back the way it was before we made the changes, there's always the chance of an accident. You might rip the hem or spill something on it. And what if Lady Florence comes home early and finds you gone? What then, Lady Francie?"

"Then I shall be sent home to Greensward in disgrace, and you will go with me," Francie pronounced, pleased with the effect of the ivory satin evening dress cut in the Empire to which she had added an overdress of white lace borrowed from Florence's wardrobe.

The décolletage, which Daisy had deepened by removing the lace fischu and trim, was far more daring than the chaste gown that had been originally designed for her coming-out ball. Even with the short, puffed sleeves that not even the cleverest seamstress could alter without permanently damaging the dress, the gown was tastefully indecent—just the sort of thing one would expect of Ransome's *inamorata,* she decided, pulling on white gloves that reached above the elbows. She would have preferred to wear diamonds, of course, but the opal pendant about her neck and the matching drops in her ear lobes were not altogether displeasing. A loo mask of white satin and lace that covered the entire upper half of her face and the application of rouge to her lips provided the crowning touches.

From her hair, worn in a chignon at the nape of the neck with tiny curls about the face, to her French-heeled white satin slippers, she was exactly what she had set out to be.

"The White Rose," Francie breathed, pleased, to herself.

At last, snatching up her ermine-lined pelisse, she turned gaily away from the looking glass. "Pray do not worry so, Daisy," Francie said, patting the frowning abigail on the arm. "No one will know, I promise. It is time for me to go now. Promise me you will be there to unlock the back door at midnight, and I shan't ask anything more of you. Remember, we are doing this for the sake of Florence's happiness."

"Oh, aye, her ladyship's happiness," Daisy answered in doleful accents. "Bringing ruin down on yourself is bound to make her happy. I daren't think what my dear mama will say when I'm sent home in disgrace."

Francie, however, had already slipped out the door and was making her way on tiptoe along the hallway to the servants' stairs. Moments later, she was safely out the back way.

A half-moon shone over the rooftops, shedding a silvery light over the stables and the carriage drive, which was noticeably empty. She wished there had been time to work out the details of her rendezvous with Ransome. Naturally, it would hardly do for him to bring his carriage into the drive, where he could not hope to escape detection by the stable lads and grooms. But then, where was he?

"Ransome," she called in a low, thrilling whisper. "My lord, where are you?"

"Here, my lady."

A tall figure loomed out of the shadows. Francie gasped.

"The devil, Ransome. You startled me."

"I beg your pardon, Lady Powell," came back to her in amused accents. "That was never my intention."

"On the contrary, my lord," Francie retorted, peering wryly up at Ransome's face, "you took great delight in it, you know you did. But at least you came. I was afraid you might have changed your mind."

"No, why should you?" queried Ransome, taking her arm and leading her along the drive to the alleyway, where a closed carriage in the care of the earl's groom awaited them. "I thought we had agreed I was a man who kept his word."

"I never doubted your word, my lord. It occurred to me that perhaps your sense of honor might have given you pause. I am not so green not to realize what it would mean if I am found out tonight."

"You reassure me, Lady Powell. I confess I did wonder if tonight's adventure was purely another case of irresistible impulse."

"Perhaps in the beginning it was, I admit," Francie said, pausing at the open door to the carriage to gaze frankly up at his lordship. "I have had considerable time for thought since last night, however, and, if you wish to bow out, I want you to know I should not hold it against you."

The devil, thought Harry, studying the lovely eyes behind the mask. What was this? Surely, the redoubtable Lady Francie was not having second thoughts. She could not possibly know how close he had come to confronting Leighton with the whole in order to put an end to the imp's ill-conceived plan. Only the utter certainty that such a move would defeat his own purposes where Lady Francie was concerned had in the end deterred him from the rational course. That, and the undeniable fact that he had found the prospect of meeting Lady Powell once more in the guise of the White Rose practically irresistible.

She had not disappointed him, he noted, keenly appreciative of the striking image of provocative beauty and pristine innocence she presented.

"You are all generosity, ma'am," Harry replied. "However, I assure you I am game if you are."

Francie expelled a sigh of relief. She had been more than a little afraid his lordship would take her up on her offer, which would have complicated things not a little. Indeed, she was not at all certain how, without him, she would have found the Goldfinch, let alone gained admittance to those forbidden premises.

"I knew you could not disappoint me," she exclaimed, awarding him a smile whose radiance would have been sufficient to spur even the least adventurous man to supreme feats of daring. "Not only are you a man of your word, my lord, but I daresay you are as keen as I to get to the bottom of this matter. I am convinced Leighton's life, not to mention my sister's happiness, depends on it."

"I should not dream of disputing the possibility, Lady Powell," Harry said, extending a hand to help her mount into the carriage before climbing in after her. "In which case, I feel I must ask that you agree to certain conditions, merely, you understand, to ensure the safe completion of tonight's venture. Come now, Lady Powell," he added, noting Francie's obvious hesitation. "You will admit that, as a soldier, I have had no little experience in covert undertakings of this sort. Surely it is not too much to ask you to trust my judgment in this matter?"

"But you must know by now, sir, that I trust you implicitly. It is only that, as a female, I am not a little experienced in being asked to adhere to conditions in all manner of undertakings, covert or otherwise. Very often I have found that such stipulations are only a not so subtle means of precluding women from all but the most innocuous aspects of participation."

"No doubt, Lady Powell," agreed Harry, reflecting that a future with Francie Powell promised to be anything but conventional. "In this case, however, you may be sure my stipulations are only what I should place on myself were I about to embark in disguise on a dangerous mission into enemy territory."

"I see," said Francie, eyeing him doubtfully. "Very well, tell me your conditions."

"When I was on reconnaissance missions behind enemy lines, I learned early on to keep a tight rein on my tongue. The less said, when one is surrounded by the enemy, the less chance of being exposed as a spy. In the circumstances, it merely occurred to me that you will be better assured of success if you present an aloof front, which means maintaining a discreet silence. There are, after all, any number of effective means of communicating without actually using one's voice, which, you will agree, might easily give you away."

"Yes, I see what you mean," said Francie, who, blessed with a vivid imagination, had little difficulty picturing Ransome, dressed in the guise of a Spanish peasant and coolly sauntering through the midst of any number of French soldiers. The image was enough to send a thrill coursing down the length of her. "Oh, but it is too marvelous. I daresay it can only add to the mystique of the White Rose. After all, what could he more intriguing than a masked woman enveloped in a mysterious curtain of silence?"

"My thoughts precisely," Harry replied with perfect gravity. "I suggest it will make the White Rose an object of endless speculation."

"She is that already, in case you had failed to notice," Francie wryly retorted. "I confess my ears have been positively burning this past week. But then, that was, of course, our object. As the White Rose, I can go without question where Francine Powell cannot."

"Which brings me to my second condition," Harry smoothly interjected. "Tonight, I should prefer that you choose to go nowhere without me, not even to mingle with the rest of the company. In fact, I believe I must insist you remain by my side at all times."

"But why?" demanded Francie, considerably taken aback at the prospect of being kept, for all practical purposes, on leading strings. "In spite of what you might think, I am perfectly capable of comporting myself in a ladylike manner. I assure you I have no intention of becoming an embarrassment to you."

"You may be equally certain that I never thought otherwise," Harry answered without the smallest hesitation. "On the other hand, to leave the mantle of my protection, even for a moment or two, would be to invite almost certain insult. In spite of my adventurous nature, I confess to finding little to recommend in the notion of a meeting at dawn. Dawn's such a blasted ungodly hour."

Francie went hot then cold at the very thought of so chilling a prospect. The possibility that Ransome might be brought to engage in a duel over her honor was simply not to be thought of. Indeed, she would never forgive herself were she to be the cause of any such thing.

"You are right, of course," she said contritely. "And I beg your pardon for misunderstanding your motives. I confess I had failed to take into account the demands on a gentleman's honor. You have my word that I shall do nothing to provoke an incident at the

Goldfinch that will cause you any unpleasantness, but you must give me yours that you will not take it upon yourself to fight for me. Not ever, Ransome. Not for something I might do. I should wish to die if anything happened to you because of me."

Harry, considerably startled by that unexpected announcement, not to mention the sincerity with which it was obviously uttered, was moved to take her hand soothingly in his. "I am gratified at your concern, Lady Powell, but it really is not necessary. Nothing is going to happen to me."

"But you cannot know that, my lord," Francie insisted distraughtly. "You do not know *me*. My mama says I am prone to cataclysmic misadventure. There is every chance I shall eventually do something that will result in an incident you might construe as grounds to call someone out, and I will not have it, Ransome. Promise me you will do nothing so utterly stupid as fight a duel over a female you cannot possibly care for, or—or—" Lifting her chin with grim determination, she finished all in a rush. "Or I fear I shall have to ask you to allow me to save Leighton all by myself."

"Then naturally I give you my word, Lady Powell," instantly agreed Harry.

Francie blinked. "You—you do?" she queried, hardly knowing whether to be relieved at his capitulation to reason or offended by the ease with which he had come to it.

"By all means, Lady Powell," replied Harry, insufferably smiling. "It would appear you leave me little choice in the matter. I can hardly allow you to deny

me the excitement of helping you track down your
murderous villains, now can I? It would go against
my natural disposition to adventure.''

"Yes, of course there is that," agreed Francie,
glancing down to hide the flash of her eyes. How
dare he view the entire venture solely as a cure for
ennui! Still, it was only what she should have expected. Nor could she blame him. After all, he was
not even acquainted with Leighton, and he could
hardly be motivated by any particular affection for
herself. Or could he? she wondered, glancing up at
his handsome profile limned against the passing
street lamps.

For the barest moment as he had held her hand,
she had seemed to sense a tenderness in his bearing
that had had little to do with his disposition to adventure. But then, very likely it had only been the
natural reaction of a generous-hearted man to her
obvious distress, she told herself, acutely aware of the
lingering warmth of his touch long after he had re-
linquished her hand.

The Goldfinch was hardly the den of iniquity that
Francie had anticipated. Far from the seedy aura of
depravity she had expected, the five-story house with
its brown brick front exuded a disappointingly quiet
elegance. Indeed, she decided, upon being admitted
by a very proper London butler, save for the marked
air of masculinity in the choice of furnishings, there
was little to distinguish it from any of the other houses
to which she and her sister had been invited for supper

and cards. But then, she had hardly expected a gaming establishment to be located in the midst of the fashionable houses on St. James's Square.

"Good evening, Pibs," Harry said to the butler, who, despite his air of preeminence, was a large, strapping man who might have stripped well in the ring. "This is my special guest whom I told you to expect."

"Madam," intoned the butler, helping Francie off with her pelisse. Francie, mindful of her promise to maintain a discreet silence, smiled and batted her eyelashes.

"Ahem!" said Pibs, clearing his throat before turning away to divest the earl of his greatcoat. The master, it would seem, had got himself a *rara avis* this time, he reflected with no little appreciation.

"I trust everything is in readiness, Pibs," said Harry, handing the butler his hat and gloves.

"Everything is just as you instructed, milord. You may be interested to know that the private saloon is presently occupied. The gentleman about whom you expressed an interest, however, has yet to put in an appearance."

"Excellent, Pibs. Be so good as to send word in the usual manner if he should arrive."

"Very well, milord," agreed Pibs, solemnly bowing.

"My dear?" Harry, smiling, offered Francie his arm.

"What gentleman?" Francie demanded as she allowed herself to be led upstairs toward a lively din of voices. "What was all that about a private saloon?"

"Softly." Harry nodded warningly to a pair of gentlemen at the head of the stairs, one of whom was eyeing him with undisguised interest. "Melcroft," he said in greeting. "Laverly. I had not thought to see you here tonight. I understood Lady Catherine was in Town."

"Oh, you may be sure of it, along with her entire cortege of cicisbeos." Laverly's handsome lips twisted in a cynical grimace. "You know how it is. Began to feel I was decidedly *de trop.*"

"Women will work havoc on a man's peace of mind, not to mention his purse," observed Melcroft sympathetically. "I say, Ransome. Could you see your way to staking me to a pony? You know I'm good for it."

Ransome, drawing a square marker from his waistcoat pocket, flipped it to the other man. "Not pockets to let at this hour, I trust?"

"Devil a bit," rumbled Melcroft, catching the marker. "The luck's bound to turn my way one of these days."

"It would appear the luck is all with Harry," commented Viscount Laverly, his gaze appreciative as it rested on the mysterious vision in white. "Going to introduce us, old man?"

"I'm afraid not, old man. My companion prefers to remain incognito." Harry, smoothly maneuvering Francie past the two, glanced briefly back over his shoulder. "The lady is Hungarian," he informed them in a carrying whisper. "Doesn't speak a word of English."

Francie smothered a gurgle of laughter. "Faith, what a whisker."

Harry grinned unrepentantly. "Yes, but admirably

suited to the purpose. And, now, perhaps you would care to meet our quarry."

Francie's heart gave a leap. "Madame Noire? Oh, but I should be ever so delighted." She glanced fleetingly about the gaming room, which, spacious and large, was occupied with any number of card tables, a layout for faro, and an E.O. table surrounded by punters and players. "Where, pray tell, is she?"

"Madame Noire fancies herself a virtuoso at Hazard, which she prefers to play in private," he informed her as they came to a pair of closed doors. "Remember, my lady," he said, touching the side of an index finger to his lips. "Not a word."

Harry reached for the door handles.

The saloon reserved for Hazard was sumptuously furnished, as befitted the dozen or more high-players seated or standing about the table. Francie's immediate impression was of oak wood paneling, a brass chandelier suspended from the ceiling over the long, rectangular playing table, and comfortable leather-upholstered armchairs. An oblong cage at one end of the table was in the process of tumbling three large dice end over end to the accompaniment of various cries from the gamesters intent on cajoling the dice to their favor.

While beside her, Ransome replied casually to greetings from various players, Francie's attention was immediately drawn to a stunning figure gowned daringly in black satin and crimson lace. Not above thirty, she was rather more voluptuous than slender and might have been described as more striking than beautiful, with china-blue eyes and jet hair, which

Francie suspected owed its inky perfection more to artifice than to nature. The only woman in the room other than Francie, she could have been no one but Madame Noire.

Behind her, one long shapely hand resting casually on the back of her chair, stood a slender gentleman remarkable for the pallor of his complexion and the thin, aesthetic cast of his features. A man in his mid to late forties, at one time he must have been thought almost Byronically handsome, but time and the ravages of vice had left their marks on him. His blond hair, crimped into waves, had begun to withdraw in the manner of a widow's peak, while deep lines reflective of cynicism had etched themselves into his face.

Strange, thought Francie, there would seem to be something about him that was vaguely familiar. But that was impossible, she told herself. She was sure she had never met the man before. His eyes lifted to survey her with indolent boldness. Francie, forcing herself to meet his gaze with a cool stare, suppressed an instinctive chill of revulsion.

Still, she must have given something away. Indeed, she could not be mistaken in thinking she had detected a sudden flicker of curiosity in the cold eyes before she glanced away.

"Sacriste!" exclaimed Madame Noire as the cage came to a stop and the banker, maintaining a stone face, raked in the square markers from the losing bets on the layout before paying off the more fortunate winners. "Another raffle. The luck is with the house tonight."

"In Hazard, the luck is always with the house, my dear," murmured the blond gentleman, leaning forward to replenish her stack of markers, considerably depleted by the previous play. "Which is why you will seldom see our friend Ransome, here, putting his blunt on the dice. A true gambler always plays the odds, does he not, my lord?"

Francie stiffened, her heart beating rapidly beneath her breast. Faith, there was no mistaking that voice. No wonder he had seemed familiar. He was the villain from the inn!

Now what the devil? Harry wondered grimly, having noted both the gentleman's deliberate appraisal of Francie and her sudden start at what would seem a harmless enough observation. There would be the bloody hell to pay if Armstead had penetrated Lady Francie's disguise. The man was as dangerous as he was addicted to vice. Significantly Harry slipped an arm about Francie's waist. "I have in general made it a rule never to gamble where the odds are against me, Armstead," he answered easily. "But then, in this case I am the house."

Francie's eyes flew to Ransome's face, then just as quickly dropped again. Little wonder Ransome was intimately acquainted with the Goldfinch and its curious history. Why the devil did he not tell her he was the proprietor?

"You see, my dear Veronique," said Armstead, his gaze, amused, on Francie, "that is precisely my point."

Madame Noire eloquently shrugged a bared white shoulder. "Yes, but what do I care for your point?

You know I play for the amusement." She laughed
and placed her markers for the next roll of the dice.

"There, you see how little my advice is regarded,"
Armstead mused plaintively, though it was clear to
Francie he did not care a whit what the lady thought
or did. "Women may always be counted on to view
the world in a different light from men. It is, is it not,
what makes them so intriguing?"

Harry smiled coldly in answer. Damn the man's
impudence. There was no mistaking whom Armstead
found intriguing. He had not taken his eyes off Francie since her arrival. If anything, his interest in the
White Rose bordered on insolence, which Harry
found puzzling in the extreme.

Armstead, the younger son of the Earl of Clarendon,
was known for his dissolute lifestyle, which had led
him to marry twice into the ranks of trade in order to
support his various vices. He likewise had been wid-
owed twice, but, presumably having been left well off
in the wake of his second wife's passing and reputed
to be Roman in his preferences, he had thus far demonstrated little inclination to the petticoat line. His
alliance with Madame Veronique Noire was accounted
as something on the order of an arrangement of convenience, though how each was profited by the other's
company had never been satisfactorily explained.
Clearly Madame Noire derived no little benefit from
Armstead's seemingly boundless purse, but what recompense she rendered unto her benefactor was nebu-
lous at best. That he should suddenly evince an
interest in another female, even one as intriguingly

mysterious as the White Rose, was consequently sufficient to arouse Harry's cautionary instincts.

"I have noticed that you never play at Hazard yourself," Harry commented, casually drawing forth an
exquisite enameled snuffbox and extracting a pinch
between thumb and forefinger. "And I have yet to
see you at bassett or faro. I have, in fact, found myself
wondering just what your game is, Armstead."

"Chess," offered Madame Noire in accents of
amusement. "Richard fancies himself a master of
chess. It is *tres amusante, non?*"

Armstead arched a single arrogant eyebrow. "You
must excuse Veronique," he drawled with his slow,
indolent smile. "Like most women, she has little understanding of what must be considered essentially a
gentleman's pastime. She is much better suited to
Hazard."

Francie's eyes glittered behind the mask. The pom-
pous prig. Not all women were suited only to the mindless game of Hazard. She felt the first stirrings of an
irresistible impulse. But, no, it would be dangerous,
and she had nothing to cover her losses if she had
overestimated her resourcefulness. And yet, what better way to learn the strengths and weaknesses of her
enemy? Had not Papa always said chess was the test of
one's mental discipline?

The next moment she was lifting her face to whisper in Ransome's ear.

Twenty minutes later, Harry was to wonder what had
possessed him to go along with what was clearly a dangerous exercise in futility, not unlike dangling a mouse
before a predatory snake, or, in this case, an infant

before a wolf. It was not that Harry begrudged the
hundred pounds used as bait to lure Armstead into a
match the man clearly viewed in the light of humoring
a presumptuous child. It was that he little liked the
notion of drawing Armstead's further attention to
Francie over the intimate width of a chessboard, not
even for the exceedingly short space of time it would
undoubtedly take for Lady Powell to go down in defeat.

The game was indeed short-lived. Lady Francie,
who, because of her gender, was graciously granted
the White, achieved checkmate in five precise moves.
It was difficult to tell who was the more astounded—
Armstead or Harry—though there was little doubt
which of them derived the greater enjoyment from
the experience.

"Impossible!" was Armstead's immediate reaction.
"I have studied all the masters since Philidor. No one
has ever begun with such a move. It was impudent
and reckless, a move only a woman would take. Furthermore, it is an opening easily thwarted. If I had
chosen to follow your pawn to queen's bishop three
with any move other than pawn to king's four, you
would not now have the victory."

Francie's answer couched in the form of a serene
smile and accompanied as it was by a delicately
smothered yawn did little to endear her to her van-
quished opponent.

Armstead's pallid cheek assumed a detectable tinge
of color.

"Hindsight is a wonderful thing, is it not?" Harry
soulfully interjected. "In point of fact, however, you

did make the move to king's four. The victory quite rightly belongs to the lady."

"Ye-es," said Armstead, drawing the syllable out. His cold gaze fixed on Francie and, like donning a cloak, he resumed his indolent front. "The proof is before us, is it not? Brava, Madame Rose. You will not, however, find me asleep a second time. The White, I believe, is mine."

The second game soon settled into a taut silence. Harry, observing from the sidelines, was keenly aware that Lady Powell, far from demonstrating any propensity for impulsive behavior, was playing with calculated precision. Indeed, it must have been as galling to Armstead as it was enlightening to Harry to discover the lady, on the defense, gave the appearance of one who knew in advance every move her opponent would make.

The denouement was as telling as it was magnificent. His white king in check for the fifth straight move and with no relief in sight, Armstead rose to his feet. "Madam," he said. "It would seem we find ourselves at an impasse. I believe I must ask if you will concede we have a draw."

Francie, who had known for some time how the game must end, graciously inclined her head. Having assessed her opponent and determined his weaknesses, she felt reasonably confident of holding her own in a third game. Indeed, with the added advantage of White, she was almost certain of winning. In spite of the fact that she could not hope to play the same opening trick on Armstead a second time or that, having been twice burned, he was not likely to underestimate her skills again, she had other surprise strategies up her sleeve. She felt her blood, swift in her veins, with a delectable sense of adventure. Indeed, she had long been aching for just such an opportunity to put her game to the touch.

So intent was she on plotting her strategy while Armstead realigned the pieces that she was hardly aware of the ringing of a small bell in one corner of the room.

Ransome, leaning with one broad shoulder propped against the wall, did not fail to notice it. The devil, he thought. It was Pibs, signaling that Leighton had arrived.

Leisurely, Harry straightened. "I'm afraid, my dear," he murmured, leaning over Francie's shoulder, "that there is not the time for another game. We must be leaving."

"Now? I wish you will not be absurd," Francie blurted. "We cannot leave now, when I—" Any further protest died on her lips at sight of the warning light in Ransome's eye. A glance at Armstead confirmed that he had heard and was regarding them both with no little interest.

A curse on the man, she thought, and smiled beatifically before rising and drawing Ransome to one side.

"The devil, Ransome, you cannot expect me to quit now, when I have every expectation of winning," she whispered fiercely in his ear, then, smiling sweetly across at Armstead, fluttered her fingers in his direction. "Besides, I have yet to learn anything other than he is as ruthless as I had reason to believe he was and that he is not nearly so adept at thinking geometrically as he imagines himself to be."

"A fatal flaw in the game of chess," observed Harry sympathetically, "but not so fatal as refusing to strategically withdraw when it is the only sure way of avoiding a rout. Leighton has just arrived."

"And if he has, surely you can keep him away." Francie grasped the lapels of Ransome's coat and tilted her head back to look up at him. "Please, Ransome. I promise I can win. Half an hour. It is all that I ask."

The devil, thought Ransome, gazing down into beautiful, entreating eyes. Never mind Leighton, it was not safe to leave her on her own with a man like Armstead for so much as a minute, let alone half an hour. It was time he reminded her of their agreement.

Harry was later to reflect that he must have suffered a momentary aberration. Certainly it was with a feeling that he had joined the ranks of bedlam that he heard himself reply, "Very well, half an hour. But no more."

"Thank you, my lord," beamed Francie, treating him to the full force of her smile. Harry's lips twisted wryly. "You will not regret it, I promise you."

"Impudent brat," Harry growled. "You may be sure that I already regret it. Half an hour," he added grimly. "I shall be outside the door, if you need me."

It came to Harry as he savagely crushed the glowing end of his second cheroot at the base of a potted fern that, as many times as he had stood watch on the Continent, he had never known time to drag so damned interminably. But then, he had not then been plagued with images of Lady Francine Elizabeth Powell alone in the company of a man who was infamous for his dissolute nature. Hell and the devil confound it! He would rather face an army of French sharpshooters than his own conscience if anything happened to the girl.

Harry's head turned at the sound of Veronique Noire's distinctively deep-throated voice, which issued from beyond the turn in the hall little more than a stride or two from where Harry stood.

"My sweet, foolish Paul, you know I am promised to Armstead tonight. No matter how much I might wish to be with you, I cannot leave him dangling."

"The devil with Armstead," growled the masculine reply, muffled, no doubt, by the speaker's lips pressed against the woman's soft, yielding flesh. "Come with me, Veronique. You know you do not care a whit for him."

"Mais non, I cannot. It would put him in a devilish fit. Tomorrow night, my darling. Ten o'clock, at the usual place. Armstead has an engagement. And you did promise to bring me something, you remember?"

"Yes, yes. The thing about Captain Norvel. I shall have it, though why you are interested in a fleet captain, I cannot imagine."

"I told you, *mon ami.* He is the friend of one of my girls. He promised to marry her. She is distracted with worry and will be of no use to me until she hears all is well with his ship. You understand."

"I understand that you are a heartless jade who delights in teasing me. Don't go, Veronique. Not yet.

Tell me about Armstead. What is this hold he has over you? It cannot be money. My purse is greater than his. Tell me, my beautiful Veronique."

A sharp gasp sounded at Harry's back. With a silent curse, he turned to find Francie, standing with her back to the door, her face nearly as white as her dress.

"Leighton," she pronounced in the barest whisper.

Harry placed a finger to his lips in silent warning.

"Stop, Paul, my darling," insisted Madame Noire beyond the corner. "You know I cannot discuss Armstead with you. I must go back. No, you go that way. We cannot be seen together, you know that."

"Quick," Harry whispered, reaching for the door handle. "Inside."

Francie fiercely shook her head. Now, what the devil? thought Harry. And where was Armstead?

The next instant, the moment for retreat was past. At the distinct tread of approaching footsteps, Harry resorted to the only stratagem open to him.

Clasping Francie savagely to his chest, he bent his head and kissed her.

No doubt it was the measure of the pitch of his emotions in the wake of an interminable half-hour of waiting for disaster to strike that he tossed aside his previous considerations for the lady's youth and untutored innocence. Aware of a pressure in his chest that had mounted with every cursed moment spent outside the oak barrier, he kissed her fully and unrestrainedly on the lips. Nor did he pause when Leighton, coming around the corner, faltered briefly before giving expression to a warning cough, followed by a gruff, "Er—beg your pardon," before proceeding on past them.

Francie, wholly unprepared for so precipitate an assault on her lips, suffered an unexpected jolt, not unlike a shock wave, which coursed through the entire length of her body arousing any number of startling physical reactions, not the least of which were a sudden giddiness, the sensation of having had a fire kindled somewhere inside her belly, and a predisposition for her knees to give way beneath her. It was certain that Ransome had her whole and undivided attention, so much so that she was completely oblivious to the fact that she was in the Goldfinch, that her brother-in-law was in the very near vicinity, or that the hall clock was striking the hour of midnight.

The sound of the marquis's footsteps had long retreated down the corridor when Harry, taking pity on the girl in his arms, at last lifted his head.

A faint smile twitched at his lips at sight of her eyes through the holes in the mask. Dazed, they stared back at him with a peculiarly fixed expression.

"Lady Powell?" he murmured gently, brushing a stray lock of hair from her cheek. "Francie."

Francie blinked. "You kissed me," she said, as though to confirm that fact in her own mind.

"It did seem like the thing to do at the time," Harry admitted without the least show of remorse. "Leighton was certain to recognize you in spite of the mask."

"Yes, I—I remember. He is gone, now. And Armstead—" She stopped, her glance going to Harry with horrified eloquence. "Dear me—Armstead!"

Harry's face underwent a grim transformation. "What about Armstead?" he demanded. "And, where, by the way, is he? If he dared so much as lay a hand on you—"

"No, no, I am perfectly all right."

"Then what—" Stopping, he gripped Francie firmly by the arms. "I'm sorry, my dear, but I'm afraid I must insist that you tell me what has happened."

"Yes, yes, though I daresay you will not like it," replied Francie, who had yet to recover from her shattering discovery that a mere kiss from Ransome was enough to transform her into something very nearly resembling a hysterical female. "Indeed, I do hope you were not overly fond of the bronze vase on the mahogany stand. I'm afraid I have put a terrible dent in it."

Harry stared at her, apparently much struck by the latent possibilities in such an admission. "The Oriental ovoid bronze with the flared lip?" he queried, arching a speculative eyebrow. The vase in question stood all of two feet five inches in height and weighed a good fifteen pounds or more.

Slowly Francie nodded. "The very one, my lord. As it happens, I'm afraid I should have listened to you. After all, I was perfectly aware that Armstead was hardly the sort to take defeat at the hands of a female with the least show of sportsmanship. In which case, I might have known he would try to snatch off my mask. I left him, sleeping it off on the Ushak rug in front of the fireplace."

"A wise decision," applauded Harry, taking her arm and starting hastily down the corridor toward his private stairs. "No doubt he will rest there comfortably enough. In the meantime, it occurs to me that we have had enough adventure for one night. It is time we were leaving."

Francie's chagrined gaze flew to Ransome as they navigated the staircase. "Ransome, we must go back. Your purse with the wager, I left it in the room with Armstead."

"The devil take the purse. At the moment, my only concern is to have you safely away from the Goldfinch before Armstead awakens."

Francie groaned to herself. Faith, how could she have forgotten the cursed money. A hundred pounds was more than her entire quarterly allowance, which she had already considerably depleted on her frequent shopping forays with Florence in Bond Street. It was not right that Ransome should be out such a sum because of her carelessness.

"I shall pay you back, my lord," Francie blurted as soon as they were alone in the carriage. "Every penny, I promise. I'm afraid, however, I find myself a trifle short of the ready. I shall have to ask you to take my marker until my next quarterly allowance."

"I haven't the least use for your money, Lady Powell," declared Harry in no uncertain terms. "It was worth a few pounds to see you take Armstead down a peg. Besides, the purse was yours. You won it. I am all curiosity to know where you learned to play chess like a master."

"It was Papa," replied Francie with a distracted wave of the hand. "An advocate of reason in all things, he preferred chess to any form of physical punishment for our childish indiscretions. I'm afraid I was his most devoted pupil. By the time I was twelve, I had learned every move Philidor ever made, not to mention those of all the lesser greats. I even developed a few strategies of my own, which was how I managed to defeat Armstead so handily in the first game. He mirrored my opening move, just as I hoped he would. After that, it was all a matter of moving the queen in for the kill. Not that it signifies. I have, after all is said and done, lost your purse for you. Really, Ransome, I must insist you allow me to pay you back. I should never forgive myself if I let you stand the nonsense."

"I told you, Lady Powell. I haven't any use for your money."

"And I tell you I cannot let you stand the nonsense. If you will not take money, then there must be something else you will accept."

"In that case, Lady Powell," said Harry, capturing her fluttering hands in his, "we shall consider the account closed. You lost my purse, and I stole a kiss. If anything, I count myself ahead in the bargain."

"A kiss." Francie, flushing scarlet beneath the mask, tried ineffectually to retrieve her hands. "I wish you will not be absurd, my lord. A kiss is hardly just recompense for a purse of a hundred pounds."

"On the contrary, Lady Powell," Harry coolly insisted. "Some kisses are beyond any price. You may be sure that, in this case, I consider myself fully recompensed."

Aware that her heart had begun to behave in a most unsettlingly erratic manner, Francie made herself laugh. "You are bamming me, my lord," she said, striving for a gay note in keeping with what she assumed was an attempt on his part at light flirtation.

Ransome, however, seemed stubbornly set on contradicting her. "I assure you I could not be more serious, Lady Powell. In fact, if you insist on paying me back, I am afraid a kiss is the only form of remuneration I am prepared to accept. That, and your promise you will not attempt anything further in the matter concerning your brother-in-law and Madame Noire without me. After tonight, I have, you will agree, a vested interest in the outcome of the game."

As they had by this time arrived in the alleyway, Francie peered at Ransome, trying to make out his face in the darkness. "You think Paul is involved in something dreadfully wrong," she said. "Pray do not deny it. I heard them, too. On the other hand, I do not believe it. No matter what we heard, I know Paul would never do anything dishonorable. There is another explanation for his odd behavior, I should stake my life on it."

"I should not be at all surprised," agreed Harry, thinking that putting her life on the line was precisely what she would be doing if she continued on her present course. What he had overheard had sounded suspiciously like treason. Stepping down from the carriage, he lifted his hand to help Francie disembark. "Have I your promise?"

Francie faced Ransome gravely. It had occurred to her that she had already asked too much of him. Not only had he forfeited a purse of a hundred pounds due to her carelessness, but it would appear that she had involved him in something a deal more serious than a mere domestic misunderstanding. If she were to tell him in addition to everything else that Armstead was the villain who had gone in pursuit of her at the inn, he would undoubtedly take it upon himself to call the man out, and that she could not allow. Even if he won such a confrontation, duelling was against the law of the realm. In which case, he would face almost certain exile.

Her mind made up, she deliberately crossed the fingers of both hands behind her back before solemnly replying, "But of course, Ransome, I promise."

Eight

Francie's repose that night was anything but restful. No matter how many sheep she counted, it was not long before a certain nobleman with eyes the penetrating blue of rapiers obtruded, wholly scattering her imaginary flock and keeping her awake.

Really, it was too bad of Ransome to play such a trick on her just when she had vowed not to make a cake of herself over him. How the devil was she supposed to maintain a cool front if at the slightest whim he decided to do something calculated to knock her off her balance?

The inescapable truth was that she could not. If nothing else, his kiss had taught her that much.

His kiss, she thought, flushing all over again from her head to her toes. If this was what it was to feel like a woman, there would seem to be a great deal left to be desired in it. No wonder Florence went around looking as if she had eaten sour apples. It occurred to Francie to wonder if her mama had ever been made to suffer the bewildering array of emotions that left one hot then cold then suddenly tingling all over. Perhaps it was something every female was forced to endure, like a curse, or like growing a bosom.

Francie had found little to recommend in reaching what her mama had described to her as being the mystical time when a girl began to undergo the transformation into womanhood. Indeed, she had come early on in the process to the opinion that females had been gypped in the grand scheme of things. Not only had she to deal with the disturbing changes in her body, which, besides occasioning her no little discomfort and inconvenience, she had neither asked for nor wanted, but she had been made to realize once and for all that she was doomed to be just like her older sisters.

It had been a lowering revelation, not because she entertained a dislike for her sisters. She had always been especially fond of Lucy at least. It was only that she had always considered their infatuation with such feminine topics as love and marriage and all the things that went with them not only silly but a ridiculous waste of time. She, after all, had no intention of ever falling in love.

Good God. No doubt it was only poetic justice that she now found herself pinioned on her own petard, she thought ruefully.

A plague on all men and Ransome most particularly! she thought, pounding a fist into her inoffensive feather pillow. She had been a fool to think for one moment she could be near Ransome and manage to remain impervious to what clearly amounted to an irresistible attraction. It came to her at last that, if she was to have any hope of retaining her dignity in an impossible situation, she must make sure never to be in his proximity again. It was not enough, after all, to refuse in future ever to waltz with him or ride again with him in a carriage. Clearly she must guard against even so much as laying eyes on him. Just to see him from across a room was enough to send her pulse skyrocketing and to cause her to experience an odd sort of quaking sensation in her extremities. If he were ever to kiss her again, she was quite certain she would simply crumble away inside like a dry biscuit.

With a groan somewhere between ecstasy and agony, Francie clutched a pillow to her breast and rolled over onto her back.

Faith, the mere thought of an existence without Ransome in it evoked a dreadful hollow sensation, like a gnawing in the pit of her stomach. Nor did it help to console herself with the assurance that it would be far better to take her bitter dose of medicine now than wait until her affliction of the heart grew to an incurable indisposition. Suffering an eternity plagued with all the symptoms of an exquisite anguish was fine in Lucy's tales of romance and horror. In real life it had all the appeal of looking forward the rest of one's life to being forced to indulge in frequent, daily doses of castor oil purely for their purgative effect.

It was not a future to contemplate with any feelings of rejoicing. It was, in fact, far better to turn her thoughts to the far more immediate problem of the plot surrounding Leighton.

Having come to the firm resolve not to involve Ransome in any further efforts to save Florence's mar-

riage, not to mention her husband, Francie was faced
with a daunting proposition. How in heaven's name
was she to discover Madame Noire's house on Swallow Street without him?

She could hardly canvas the entire length of the
street in search of the right house. The very idea was
patently absurd. Equally impossible was the notion of
making inquiries among her various new acquaintances. Even if there had been one among them who
had heard of Madame Noire, it would hardly be to
Francie's credit to be asking questions about a female
who was undoubtedly a member of the muslin set. If
it did not ruin Francie's standing, it would at the very
least get back to Florence, and that would never do.
Florence was not above sending her home out of the
belief it was for Francie's own good.

Still, there must be a way, mused Francie, flopping
over on her stomach. If Leighton had indeed gotten
himself in the clutches of a spy ring, she must be willing to go to any lengths to gain admittance to the
house on Swallow Street. No doubt Madame Noire
kept a wall safe or some such thing in which there
might be stored any number of incriminating documents. And there was always the chance she might be
able to overhear something, she reflected, visualizing
herself concealed behind a window drape with Armstead and Madame Noire only a few feet away in the
act of plotting some new move in their sinister game.

It was simply too delectable, she thought, an adventure to curl one's toes. And if Ransome could not be
there to share it, at least she could console herself with
her single, most important discovery. She at least knew

what Ransome did not. Madame Noire, while undoubtedly dangerous, was obviously only a tool.
Armstead was the real key to the plot.

Briefly she toyed with the idea of setting up a flirtation with Armstead. He had, after all, displayed a certain interest in the White Rose. Or at least he had until
she had been forced to resort to violent means of persuasion to protect the secret of her identity from him.
She doubted not that he would like very much to get
his hands on her, but hardly for any purpose other
than to wring her neck.

All of which left her without a single viable option.
Or at least none that she could think of at the present,
she reminded herself. No doubt *something* would
come to her on the morrow. Papa always said there
was not a problem that did not have some sort of solution if one was only willing to reason the thing
through.

Having thought the matter through until she was
utterly exhausted, Francie fell at last into a restless
slumber in which her dreams were disturbed by vi-
sions of Ransome bearing the White Rose away on a
grey charger.

The next morning Florence was moved to observe
as they met for breakfast that Francie appeared to
have little benefited from an evening at home.

"You look positively hagged," she said, pressing the
back of her hand to her sister's forehead. "I do hope
you are not coming down with something. It would
never do to be ill and confined at home, now of all

times. Need I remind you that your ball is less than a week away?"

"You have reminded me of it any number of times," Francie retorted with something less than her usual good humor. "I wish you will not hover over me, Flo. You know I am never ill."

"Well, it is obvious something is the matter," observed Florence, carefully seating herself at the breakfast table. She was afraid she knew very well what the matter was. Francie displayed all the signs and symptoms of a woman in love. "Is there perhaps something you would wish to tell me, Francie?" she ventured after a moment as she stirred sugar into her coffee. "I promise I am perfectly willing to listen."

Francie, touched by what gave every evidence of sincerity on Florence's part, suffered a swift pang of conscience. Perhaps she should tell Flo what she suspected. Florence was Leighton's wife, after all. She had a right to know if her husband was making a perfect idiot of himself over a woman who was not worth Flo's little finger. If anyone could woo him away from Madame Noire, surely it was Florence herself. Indeed, it occurred to her suddenly that perhaps Florence *was* the solution to the problem.

"Really, Flo, I haven't the least notion what you mean," declared Francie, crossing to fill a plate at the sideboard. "Heavens, what could there be? I am, after all, the second most talked about female in London. I have been swamped with calling cards from importunate suitors who are positively bereft at the news that I am indisposed. Lord Albermarle has claimed he will storm the bastions if I remain over-long in my fortress."

"Albermarle!" exclaimed Flo, giving a startled choke. "Good heavens, he is sixty if he is a day. Pray don't tell me he has joined the ranks of your admirers."

Francie shrugged an indifferent shoulder. "I only know that his card was among those that were delivered here yesterday afternoon, and that was the message scribbled on the back. I daresay his is only a passing fancy. According to Miss Wilmington, he is not the sort to marry."

"No, I should say not, at his age, though one never knows. He is a charming ne'er-do-well whose only redeeming characteristics are his willingness to stand up with matrons and aging spinsters and an inexhaustible supply of anecdotes about practically anyone one would care to name. I suppose he came hoping for some juicy tidbit about the female for whom Ransome dared the hallowed halls of Almack's. I daresay he is harmless enough if you do not make the error of confiding in him too freely."

"Then you may be sure I shall guard my tongue around him," promised Francie, who had just conceived of another use for Lord Albermarle. "How did you find Lady Trowbridge's soiree?" she queried next, casually changing the subject. "Did the Rumanian prince cut a dashing figure?"

"I should say he was more dipped than dashing, though his figure was well enough. He seemed to spend an inordinate amount of time around the punch bowl." Laying the spoon aside, Flo took a sip of her coffee. "I daresay you will have a chance to discover what he is like for yourself. I understood that he was promised to Lady Desborough's masqued ball tonight. A pity Leighton will not be there to see it," she added, staring into the black swirl of coffee. Then, as though shaking off a melancholy thought, she glanced, smiling up at Francie. "It is to have an Egyptian theme, did you know? Lady Desborough was boasting that they had gone to a shocking expense to transform the ballroom into an oasis, complete with palm trees and a miniature replica of a watering hole. Absurd, is it not?" She set the cup down. "I daresay Leighton would have derived no little amusement from the sight of Lady Desborough in the guise of a Cleopatra. I can almost hear what he would say—that with her poisoned tongue, no doubt she had done better to go as the asp."

As this last was uttered in something on the order of a shrieking gasp, Florence clapped a hand to her mouth. Hastily she turned her face away. Like a toy that had been wound too tight, she appeared suddenly to break.

For once in her life, Francie was too stunned to speak. For what seemed an endless moment, but could not have been more than a few seconds at best, the two girls sat in wretched silence, Florence, weeping silently, her shoulders shaking, and Francie, feeling miserably at a loss as to what to do or say. Trying to think what Lucy, as the eldest, or even Josephine, as the one blessed with a sympathetic insight, would do in such a situation availed her nothing. In the end, she could only do what came naturally to her.

Stepping around the corner of the table, she thrust a linen napkin at Florence. "For God's sake, Flo. Enough is enough. If you are going to turn into a watering pot, I shall think you a dreadful bore. And don't even think of falling into a fit of the sullens and running off as you did the last time, or I promise I shall lose all patience with you."

Florence, who might have expected a more sympathetic reaction from one who was, after all, one of her closest kin, was startled by that heartless pronouncement into giving vent to a watery hiccough.

"No doubt—I'm sorry—to make such a dis—play of myself," she said resentfully between convulsive sniffs and shuddering gasps.

"Gammon. You are not in the least sorry. You have been playing the wounded martyr ever since I arrived. Now you will stop your crying and blow your nose, after which we shall sit down and you will tell me why you and Leighton are behaving like two characters in a French comedy."

Florence, manifesting the aspect of one who had just received a cold dash of water in the face, glared at Francie. Then just as suddenly as she had given way to tears, she gave into a reluctant grimace and, snatching the napkin from Francie, fiercely blew her nose into it. "Repellent brat," she sniffed. "I cannot imagine how Mama puts up with you. You are utterly without the finer feelings."

"Cloth-head," retorted Francie, grinning in manifest relief. "It is time you stopped playing the grand marchioness and started being yourself. I daresay if

Mama were here, she would read you a curtain lecture on the subject."

"If Mama were here, she would give you a mountain of mending to do to cure you of your impertinence. Faith, how I miss her. And Papa. Sometimes I wish I had never left Greensward."

"I daresay we all shall have to leave it at some time or other," Francie said wistfully, "if only to learn how dear it has been to us. Naturally, I shall be going back to it, but you, my goosish older sister, must create a Greensward of your own. I should think half a dozen Moberlys should do for a start."

Francie, watching her sister's reaction to that prescription for what ailed Flo, waited, half-expecting that she had gone too far. She was no little surprised, therefore, when Florence merely sighed and, rising from the table, crossed to gaze out the window on to the cottage garden at the back of the house.

"You cannot know how I have missed the country," she said quietly, after a moment. "This is all I have of it, a small plot of garden flowers, and do you want to know what I find so dreadfully amusing about it?" She glanced briefly over her shoulder at Francie, then swiftly away again. "When I married Paul, I thought I should have everything I ever wanted—position, influence, the opportunity to be the most celebrated hostess in the *ton*. I wanted to fling it all back in their faces—all the Lady Desboroughs who turned up their noses at me because I made the supreme error of not taking my first Season. Faith, how I despised them. I was Lady Florence Powell. My father was the Earl of Bancroft, but it was not enough. Do

you know I actually blamed Papa because he chose
to lead the life of a country squire in, of all places,
the North Yorks?" She gave a small, bitter laugh. "He
might as well have been a Nobody for all the good
he did me. Or so I told myself. And Lucy. Faith, how
could anyone hope to compete with the Duchess of
Lathrop? The irony is she could not have cared less
whether she was a success or not. She had Phillip,
and that was all that mattered to her."

Francie, who had had to bite her tongue to keep
from blurting something out that must have been certain to interrupt her sister's train of thought, caught
her breath as Florence turned to look at her.

"I could not understand that. She had everything
I wanted, everything I thought would come to me—
all those years of waiting for my time, my Season in
London, my triumph. Lucy had it all, and it meant
nothing to her."

"Yes, but you know Lucy," Francie said with a helpless gesture of the hand. "She probably never even
noticed that everyone was making a fuss over her. I
daresay she saw it all merely in the light of research
for another of her novels."

Francie was about to add that Florence should try
and put it all in the past, that, after all, she had got
what she wanted. Then it came to her that Florence
had not been attending.

"I was wrong, Francie, about everything," Florence
stated flatly. "It was never what I wanted, only I was
too stupid to see it until it was too late. I would trade
it all just to have Paul back again, to have him look at
me the way he did at the beginning. He is all I have

ever wanted or shall ever want again. And the really funny thing is I do not even know what I did to lose him.''

Nine

It occurred to Francie that there was something to be said for the custom of draping oneself from head to toe in a concealing veil, though she certainly could find little in it to recommend on a long-term basis. It would, after all, tend to become a dreadful nuisance when riding neck or nothing on a swift horse, and it would be most annoyingly in the way in the event one wished to engage in any sort of meaningful conversation. Furthermore, besides tickling one's face, the thing had a tendency to stifle one's breathing, not to mention the freedom of movement. Still, she could not have asked for a better means of achieving complete anonymity, which suited her purposes very well for the evening.

Florence aside, Francie doubted there was a soul present at Lady Desborough's masqued ball who guessed her identity, let alone that she was wearing, concealed beneath her flowing Egyptian costume, a modest round gown of grey serge, borrowed after a deal of persuasion from Daisy. A white cap, shawl, and a pair of lace-up half-boots would be added later, if everything went according to plan. In the meantime, she could only hope that Wiggens did not show craven.

The old family groom was the one weak link in her carefully thought-out strategy. Everything else had fallen into place with unbelievable facility.

She could only account it a rare stroke of good fortune that Lord Albermarle had proven uncommonly firm in his resolve to make her acquaintance. He had presented his card at her door at precisely eleven o'clock that morning. It was equally fortunate she had had Daisy in attendance in lieu of Florence, who had left on her round of morning calls, leaving Francie with strict instructions to rest. A lively half-hour of avoiding the old roue's practiced attempts to corner her on the sofa, the love-seat, or the chair had ensued, during which she had managed with great finesse to garner some interesting, if somewhat puzzling, tidbits of information.

Madame Veronique Noire, it would seem, was not wholly bereft of the finer instincts. She might present the appearance and even the behavior of a woman of questionable morals, but beneath the brass exterior, there must have beat a heart with at least a smidgen of gold. Why else, after all, would she have opened her home to itinerant, unemployed actresses in need of a roof over their heads?

Francie's mama had always said that every soul had a spark of good in it; one had only to look for it. In this case, Francie could only be glad that Madame Noire's aberrant spark of generosity offered a perfect excuse to gain admittance to the boarding house for actresses without having to resort to actual breaking and entering.

Having gone over each step of her plan once again in her mind, Francie turned her attention outward to the ball going forth around her. Florence had not exaggerated when she said Lady Desborough had spared no expense to replicate a desert oasis, though Francie rather doubted many watering holes came complete with a spouting fountain, not to mention a wall mural in the background, presumably of the pyramids at Gizeh. The oddity of potted palms waving overhead must have cost her a small fortune. Humorously, Francie wondered if the tall Bedouin sheik standing picturesquely beneath one of them, his face except for his eyes covered, was meant to be one of the props. Certainly in his long flowing headdress, one corner draped across his face below the eyes, and white robes, he presented the perfect romantic complement to his surroundings.

Hardly had that thought crossed her mind, when she became aware that the tall stranger was staring back at her with what gave every manifestation of keen interest. Unaccountably, her heart gave a leap as she beheld him start toward her with unmistakable deliberation.

The devil, she thought. It was almost ten—time to make her retreat out the back way. The last thing she wished at the moment was to attract anyone's notice.

She glanced away, pretending an interest in the dancers. Then casually, so as not to appear to be fleeing, she strolled through the French doors behind her and out onto the terrace. She was just congratulating herself on having made her escape; indeed, she had reached a section of the terrace wall bathed in deep shadows and was contemplating hiking one leg over it with the intent of scaling it, when she was stopped in her tracks by a pointed "Ahem!" issuing from behind her.

Giving vent to a low gasp, she spun about—and was met with the sight of her Bedouin pursuer, leaning with his back against the wall, his arms folded across his chest, and apparently contemplating the moonlit vista before him.

"Faith," she exclaimed, clasping a hand over her breast.

"A beautiful evening, is it not?" replied the sheik soulfully. "I daresay you, too, felt an irresistible impulse to go for a stroll in the moonlight. I am not intruding, am I?"

Francie suffered an immediate sinking sensation in the pit of her stomach. Ransome! Faith, she might have known.

"As a matter of fact, you are, my lord," she declared baldly, having immediately discarded the vain notion that he was unaware of who she was. "How the devil did you know?"

"No doubt I have an uncanny ability for penetrating disguises," he reflected whimsically, uncovering his face. "He is not coming, by the way. I took the liberty of having him waylaid."

"You may be blessed with a gift for the uncanny, my lord," Francie retorted testily. "I, unhappily, am not. Who is not coming?"

"Your groom, of course. Wiggens, is that his name?

A crusty old fellow, who probably knows more about cattle than most men have forgotten. He and I had a long talk last night after you went inside."

Francie's head came around. "How very nice for you," she said sweetly. "And I suppose you spent the whole time talking about horses?"

The handsome lips curved in a slow smile that did unseemly things to Francie's interior organs. "Actually, you were the main topic of conversation. I am happy to say you have a good friend in Wiggens."

"You hardly need to tell me about Wiggens," Francie retorted testily. "As it happens, he has been with us forever. He put me on my first horse."

"So he did not hesitate to inform me. As a matter of fact, he took no little pride in it."

Francie flushed, feeling Ransome's eyes on her. "Naturally, he would," she said grudgingly. "What else did he tell you? That I am forever landing myself in one scrape after another? It is true, you know."

"I believe he did mention something about Lady Francine's high spirits. But then, you yourself took great pains last night to enlighten me as to your proclivity for cataclysmic misadventure. It seems Wiggens was witness to our little rendezvous. Consequently, it will hardly surprise you to learn he was waiting up to see you made it home safely."

"No, it is only what I should expect of him," Francie agreed, feeling a lump rise in her throat at the thought of her old servant's loyalty. That he had not gone to Florence with the tale was typical, as well. Wiggens had practically made a career of covering for Francie since the time she had snuck into the stables at the age of

eleven and stolen a ride on Bellerophon, her papa's
mettlesome stallion. Still, Wiggens might have told
Francie herself that he had spoken with Ransome, she
reflected, nettled in spite of herself with the old
groom. After all, since Ransome obviously knew what
she had intended for this evening, Wiggens must have
been the one to tell him. Really, it was the shabbiest
thing. "The two of you cooked this up together," she
said, everything having been made suddenly perfectly
clear to her. "Didn't you? It is a fine thing when I
cannot trust my own servants anymore. What, precisely, did you do, my lord, to turn him against me?"

A glint, distinctly ironic, flickered in Harry's eyes.
"Nothing much. I found him an easy mark. I had
only to convince him that I was your friend and that,
as your friend, I had every intention of looking out
for your best interests."

Francie bit her lip in chagrin. Damn Ransome, anyway. "I suppose I deserve that, for thinking the worst
of Wiggens. Still, you had no right to use him against
me, my lord." Francie's chin came up. "I—I should
have expected better from a gentleman of honor."

"Then no doubt I should beg your pardon," observed Harry, studying the well-manicured nails of a
strong, shapely hand. "Naturally, I shall refrain from
mentioning the promise you gave me. It was obvious
you had never the least intention of keeping it.
Which, by the way, is why I needed Wiggens to keep
me informed of your movements."

Francie's eyes widened in the slit between the headdress and veil. "You had him spy on me? *Wiggens?*"
she demanded in no little amazement. Turning, she

paced a step, only to come immediately back again. "The devil. Next I suppose you intend to inform me that my sister is in on this conspiracy, too."

Harry shrugged broad shoulders. "I hardly think the marchioness would view an excursion to Lady Noire's in the proper spirit of adventure. However, if you think she would like to come along, I suppose you could invite her. Of course, there is always the possibility that—"

Whatever possibilities he envisioned in such an invitation were to remain forever unstated.

Francie, giving a shriek, launched herself against his chest. "Ransome," she exclaimed, clasping her arms ingenuously about his neck. "You mean to take me to Madame Noire's boarding house! Oh, I could almost forgive you the shabby trick you played on me. Indeed, if I were not perfectly furious with you for corrupting Wiggens, I should feel like hugging you."

Harry, who was acutely aware that she was giving a fair imitation of just such an embrace and further that he was deriving no little pleasure from it, wisely forbore from drawing her attention to those pertinent facts. Not a little experienced in the art of love, he was all too aware that he had come perilously close the night before to frightening her away with a kiss that had awakened her not only to herself, but to the latent possibilities in himself. While he could only be gratified by her sweet, unbridled response, it behooved him to proceed with caution for a time.

"Madame Noire's boarding house, did you say?"

he queried instead, a single arrogant eyebrow sweeping upward toward his hairline.

"Madame Noire's boarding house for itinerant actresses who have the misfortune to be unemployed," Francie expanded. "But then, you did not know, did you? Lord Albermarle was kind enough to tell me all about it."

Lord Albermarle, good God! thought Harry. The marchioness would seem to have an odd notion of the proper company for her sister to keep. "Including, one must suppose, the direction."

"Well, naturally, Ransome. How do you suppose I meant to find it?"

"I should have thought you would come to me. That, I must suppose, however, never occurred to you."

"Dear, you are angry, are you not," observed Francie, withdrawing her arms from about his neck in order to study his face. "No doubt I am sorry I decided to exclude you from tonight's adventure. On the other hand, I did it for your own good. After all, it did not seem quite right to involve you in what might very well turn out to be far more dangerous than you had any cause to expect. It is not as if you are a particular friend of Leighton's. I fear I could not see the least reason why you should wish to involve yourself any further."

"I am well aware that you cannot," Harry said in exceedingly dry tones. "On the other hand, I have every expectation of amending that situation before very much longer. Until then, I shall thank you to allow me in future to decide what is for my own good. Now, however," he added, vaulting lightly to the top of the terrace wall and extending a hand down to her, "I suggest, if we are to have you back before you are missed, we continue this discussion in our waiting conveyance."

Swallow Street, running roughly parallel to Bond Street to the west, was a dingy, irregular thoroughfare remarkable for its filth and squalor. Indeed, it was difficult for Francie to accept that the sumptuous environs of Mayfair and Bond Street should flourish adjacent to the maze of dirty tenements and close, dark narrow alleyways, which riddled the Soho district and Leicester Square like so many rat warrens. She could not quell a shudder of horror at the miserable creatures huddled in doorways or slouching along the streets, far too many of them children. There had never been anything like this in the North Yorks. Even the meanest cottage there had the advantages of fresh air and sunlight, not to mention the ever-present garden and vegetable patch.

"Not quite what you expected, Lady Powell?" queried Harry, hunched over the reins of the tired old hack drawn by an equally decrepit grey gelding. Having discarded his flowing robes for a ragged greatcoat and slouch hat, pulled down low over his forehead, there was little in his slumped figure to recall the rakish Earl of Ransome. "But then, adventures very often have their seamier side. Take that stable, for instance. No doubt you would be interested to know it is a notorious rendezvous for highwaymen. Jack Cates himself has been known to frequent it."

"No doubt I should be properly impressed by that information," replied Francie, hugging the tattered woolen coat closer about her shoulders. A disreputable garment, it, along with scuffed shoes and a hat that could never have laid the smallest claim to anything remotely resembling beauty, had been provided her through Ransome's thoughtful generosity. "Unfortunately, I have never heard of Jack Cates."

Harry, flicking the reins, clicked his tongue at the plodding beast. "Jack Cates is only the most notorious highwayman ever to operate out of London. Known affectionately as Laughing Jack, he may be identified by his quirkish tendency to giggle during the act of robbing his victims."

"Giggle?" exclaimed Francie incredulously. "What a corker. You are obviously roasting me, Ransome"

"Not at all, Lady Powell," Harry objected. "Would I lie to you?"

"Only if it suited your purposes," Francie retorted, eyeing him sagely.

Harry grimaced. "Impudent brat. Obviously you haven't the least respect for your elders."

"Only if they are very old and decrepit," Francie replied sweetly. "In your case, I should give it another year or two. Now pray get on with your story. Why did Cates give way to the giggles?"

"No one knows, though, personally, I suspect it was the result of a nervous disorder."

"Indeed," smiled Francie, marveling at Ransome's vivid imagination. "Or perhaps he is only a jolly little fellow."

"There is always that possibility. But then, how did you guess?" Harry asked in apparent surprise.

"Guess?" demanded Francie, nettled. "Guess what?"

"Why, that Laughing Jack is possessed of a diminutive stature. Besides being prone to the giggles, he has the added distinction of standing little taller than waist-high to an average-sized man."

Francie eyed Ransome with no little incredulity. "Good God, a dwarf. Now you *are* bamming me, Ransome. I find it difficult to believe a man the size of a small child could make a successful career out of robbing coaches. It is too absurd by half."

"I never said he was successful," replied Harry, who gave every impression of a man in dead earnest. "Only that he is notorious. As it happens, I know of only one instance when he was able to escape with the goods. A draper, caught out in a downpour with a wagon loaded with bolts of crimson satin. Intended, it is said, for a casket maker, I have no doubt it was to be used as lining for coffins."

"Oh, no doubt," agreed Francie, hard put not to give way to mirth. "You were saying about the draper?"

"Ah, yes. The poor man, blinded by the storm, heard Laughing Jack's giggle and, mistaking it for the demented cackle of a disembodied spirit, or an escaped Bedlamite at the very least, fled willy-nilly, leaving Jack the spoils. I have it from a reliable source that the ladies in the vicinity of that particular stable have been known ever since as the Scarlet Women of Swallow Street."

"Oh, I am sure of it," gurgled Francie, her eyes overbrimming with laughter. "And Jack? What became of him?"

"He has not been heard of since. I like to think, however," Harry mused whimsically, "that he has found a new means of support, one which has proven far more lucrative for him than thievery."

"Faith, what a Banbury story. One day I shall have to introduce you to my sister Lucy. No doubt the two of you should rub along famously. She happens to be a writer of romance stories."

"Be certain that I shall hold you to that," said Harry, turning the grey into a deserted lot filled with rubble. "I have a particular wish to meet the woman capable of legshackling Lathrop. In the meantime, it would seem prudent to leave our conveyance here. As it happens, the house is on the next corner."

Francie started, made aware by that announcement that she had been so utterly distracted by the tale of Laughing Jack Cates as to forget all about her surroundings, which, had she stopped to think about it, must have been Ransome's intent all along.

The neighborhood in which she found herself was somewhat less rundown than those through which they had earlier passed, she noted, as she waited for Ransome to tie up the gelding. There was, in fact, a certain seedy charm to the brown brick three-story Georgian houses, lining the street on both sides. No doubt at one time they had been the homes of moderately successful tradesmen. Now, they bore the unmistakable signs of wear and neglect.

"I still cannot think why you will not at least consider my proposal," whispered Francie, as Ransome, warning her to stay close, made for the alleyway at the back of the houses. "I daresay I should have little difficulty passing as a potential lodger."

"You may be sure you would pass with flying colors," Harry said, picking his way through the garbage strewn in the alleyway. "One look at you, and they would undoubtedly welcome you with open arms."

"Well, then?" Francie demanded, nettled by something in Ransome's tone which hinted at something he was not telling her. "Pleading weariness after a long journey from the country, I shall ask to be shown to a room. Once I am alone, I shall steal into Madame Noire's private quarters. She, after all, will be off somewhere with Leighton. It is all very simple and straightforward. I fail to see any reason why you should dismiss it out of hand."

"It is obvious, is it not?" said Harry, who had *every* reason to deplore such a madcap scheme, not the least of which was the utter certainty that she had not the slightest notion into what she would be getting herself. That, and the fact that he was not prepared yet to disabuse her of her illusions so long as there was the slimmest chance of avoiding it. "I must naturally object to any scheme designed to deprive me of my share of the adventure. Either we do the thing together, or we do it not at all. Besides," he added, hoping to appeal to her sense of daring, "where would the fun be in going through the front door, when we might scale the drainpipe and break in through a window?"

Francie frowned, thinking that Ransome had failed

to grasp the obvious. The best hope of success in any undertaking must always be the one with the fewest complications. Still, she could hardly deny that it would be exceedingly selfish of her to exclude him from an active part in a dangerous mission. He was, after all, a soldier. He would naturally object to being left to cool his heels in a place of safety, while she took all the risks.

She could hardly have guessed that Harry, far from relishing the adventure afoot, was heartily wishing Madame Noire, not to mention Leighton, to the devil. He entertained a particular aversion to the notion of scaling the side of a three-story house in the dead of night in the company of a female who should by all rights have been dancing the waltz instead of flirting with what he privately considered a pointless exercise in danger. There was, after all, less than one chance in a thousand that hardened spies would keep incriminating evidence lying around.

Having repeatedly chided himself for a fool, he comforted himself with the knowledge that he had every intention in the very near future of bringing Lady Powell's career in espionage to a complete and sudden end. With that, and the fact that Harry, upon receiving word from Wiggens detailing Lady Francie's newest start, had taken the precaution of reconnoitering the grounds. He, consequently, had the advantage not only of knowing the exact location of Madame Noire's private suite of rooms, but of having ascertained the safest point of entry. The latter was in truth a drain-pipe of heavy lead, which, fastened securely to the back of the house, passed within inches of Madame Noire's bedroom window.

The ascent was easily accomplished. Harry, going first, made short work of forcing the window up. Swinging a leg over the sill, he was soon in a position to pull Francie in behind him.

Kneeling, he thrust his head and shoulders out the window. Only Francie was not on the drainpipe.

Lady Powell was nowhere in sight.

Ten

"Well, what have we here?" crooned Veronique Noire, surveying Francie's stiffly defiant figure, clutched ignominiously, her feet off the floor, between two grinning brutes.

"An actress, lookin' for lodging, or so she claims t' be," guffawed one of the brutes who apparently answered to the name of Ralph.

"Caught her sneaking around outside," vouchsafed the other, a Dinkerly Dan, or some such thing. "Fought like a bloomin' hellcat, she did."

"It was only what you deserved, you gape-toothed mental defective," Francie declared heatedly.

"Ah, now," jeered Dinkerly Dan, thrusting his face to within inches of Francie's. "No need t' be unpleasant. Was you nice t' me, might be you and me could become jolly good friends."

As this was accompanied by a strong emanation of sour breath, not to mention other unpleasant aromas, Francie naturally took exception to both the brute and his offer.

"Why, you malodorous overgrown primate. Put me *down!*" Breaking into a furious struggle, she twisted and turned, her feet kicking wildly at the two men who held her.

Madame Noire smiled in chilly amusement, apparently content to watch the captive's valiant efforts to dislodge herself at the painful expense of her two abductors, until at last it seemed that the girl might actually injure herself before giving in to the inevitable.

"Enough!"

Francie, recognizing the uncompromising voice of command, went instantly still, her breast heaving from her vigorous exertions.

"Yes, that's more like it," said Madame Noire.

Reaching for a cigarillo on a desk behind her, she cut off the tip, then leaned down to light it off a smoking oil lamp. She drew deeply and exhaled a thick, grey cloud before turning her attention back to her glaring captive.

"Release her," she commanded, and with long, painted fingernails delicately picked a speck of tobacco off the tip of her tongue and flicked it away.

Ralph and Dinkerly Dan, taking her literally at her word, dropped their troublesome burden without further adieu.

Francie landed on her posterior with a painful thump on the floor. "The devil," she uttered, her legs sprawled out before her. Savagely, she thrust the hair out of her face. "If this is the way you treat all the young women who come to you in search of a room, I daresay you have a dearth of boarders. What kind of a boarding house is this?"

"Boarding house?" Madame Noire elevated a carefully plucked eyebrow. "What kind of a boarding house do you think it is?"

Francie, sliding her heels up next to her smarting derriere, shoved herself with her hands to her feet. "I was told," she said, dusting herself off, "you took in unemployed actresses in need of a roof over their heads."

"Oh, aye," chortled one brute to the other, "a boarding house for actresses. That's what it be."

"Silence!" With a curt thrust of her chin, Madame Noire dismissed the two henchmen, who departed, leering at Francie. Her gaze speculative on her uninvited guest, Madame Noire elegantly draped her buxom figure over a rolled-arm couch.

Francie, who could not but be keenly aware that Ransome must surely be in the adjoining room with his ear to the door, stared back at her in fascination. Scantily clad in a black gauze peignoir through which could clearly be seen a black leather-and-lace corset and short black bloomers, not to mention black net stockings held in place with beribboned garters, Madame Noire hardly had the look of one anticipating the arrival of a gentleman caller.

With a pang of alarm, Francie wondered why the woman was not at her tryst with Leighton.

"Is that what you are, an actress?"

The question, couched in insinuating tones, issued from behind a trailing spiral of smoke.

"It's what I hope to be," Francie answered. She gazed frankly about her at the garishly furnished apartment, which appeared to do double duty as a study and sitting room. "It's why I ran away from home. You're the picture of everything I should imagine it to be. I've never seen anyone who looked quite like you. Is it wonderful, the stage?"

"But of course." Madame Noire's throaty laugh, Francie noted, would seem to say otherwise. Indeed, there was a great deal about Madame Noire and her surroundings that was puzzling. But then, no doubt any boarding house for actresses would have a tendency to appear somewhat out of the ordinary. The stage probably lent itself to strange bedfellows.

Madame Noire lifted a languid hand and traced a pirouette in the air. "Turn, turn. Let me have a look at you. *Deucement, mademoiselle.* If you are to be an actress, you must learn to move with elegance and grace. Not *gauche,* like a milkmaid. A man's eyes will not follow a milkmaid."

"Is that important?" asked Francie, assaying to give her best imitation of a ballerina mincing about in clodhoppers.

"You ask too many questions," snapped Madame Noire. "Stop. Stop." Rising from the couch, she approached Francie. "You move like a great oaf of a bear. Still, I see some possibilities." Picking up a handful of Francie's hair, she let it slide from her fingers in a shimmering cascade. The plucked eyebrow shot instantly upward again, followed by a sudden narrowing of the hard, painted eyes on Francie's unblemished features. "Let me see your hands," she snapped.

Reluctantly, Francie extended the requested members.

Madame Noire, snatching them up, studied the

backs, then turned them over to look at the palms. At sight of the calluses, which, the result of endless hours spent riding and working her horses, Francie's mama had always deplored, Madame Noire appeared suddenly to relax. "You should not chew your nails," she pronounced shortly. Releasing Francie, she turned away.

Francie, sensing she had just narrowly passed a test of some sort, released a slow, silent breath. "I do try, but it is a habit. I never seem quite able to break it."

"You will break it, I will see to that. For now, you will be taken to a room, where you will change into the clothes you are given. There is one rule only: You will do exactly as you are told. Always. Do you comprehend?"

"Does this mean you are giving me lodging?" queried Francie, lifting her eyebrows.

Madame Noire crossed to yank on a bellpull.

"Why not?" Veronique shrugged. "I am feeling generous tonight. You will have a room for as long as you do as you are told. If you fail in that regard, even so much as to talk back to me, you will be made instantly to regret it. Remember that. But wait. You must have a name." The woman appeared to reflect, her gaze appraising Francie, rather as if she were some sort of stray cat that had just wandered in. Still, she supposed all actresses had to have some sort of a stage name. "You will be Lily. Yes, it suits you," she added in apparent satisfaction, then turning away, called out in answer to a timid rap on the door, "Yes, yes. Come in."

An overly slender girl with dark hair and grave eyes

too old for her face entered, dressed in the garb of
a maidservant.

"This is Lily," Madame Noire declared, gesturing
with a dismissive hand toward Francie. "She is to have
Flora's room. See that she is properly gowned, and
then come back to me. I have decided to go out."

"Yes, madam." The girl bobbed a curtsey.

Francie, realizing she had been summarily dismissed, gave a last glance around the room in search
of the most likely place for a wall safe, then, congratulating herself on having so easily achieved the first
phase of her plan, followed the girl out of the room.

As her earlier entrance into the house had been
unceremonious at best, Francie had received only the
vaguest impression of red paperhangings, a red
Aubusson carpet, and the distinct sounds of voices,
both male and female. Indeed, it had occurred to her
just before she was thrust bodily into Madame Noire's
presence that there was some sort of entertainment
in progress.

The dimly lit halls were quiet now, save for an occasional feminine giggle issuing from behind one or another of the closed doors, which lined the hall on both
sides. Peculiarly, these were often accompanied by a
distinct rumble of masculine mirth.

Francie, who was beginning to think there was
something definitely havey-cavey about Madame
Noire's boarding house, turned her attention to the
girl at her side.

"My name isn't really Lily," she offered confidingly.

The girl gave Francie a queer look, but vouchsafed
no other response.

Nettled, Francie tried again. "I suppose Lily's as good a name as any other. What's yours?"

"They calls me Philomene. My real one bain't near so nice. Here we be, miss." Philomene, opening a door, let Francie go in, before following to light a lamp.

Paperhangings of a blushing rose leaped out at Francie, along with a dressing table littered with crystal bottles, satin drapes, a flowered carpet, a settee, and a wardrobe, all done in a shade of pink, which Francie mentally labeled "putrid." It was the bed, however, which attracted Francie's immediate attention.

Canopied and lavishly draped in satin and velvet of the same hue as the rest of the furnishings, it dominated the room, a pink pillowed monstrosity of queenly proportions. Francie had never before seen such a bed.

It struck her with horrid significance that no respectable boarding house for actresses or anyone else, for that matter, would have furnished such a bed, not to mention its exotic surroundings, save for one purpose only.

"Good God," she breathed, struck with instant realization. This was no boarding house, and Veronique Noire was hardly a kind-hearted philanthropist. The woman was the madame of a bordello, and she, Lady Francine Elizabeth Powell, presumably was about to make her debut as one of Madame's girls! It was all simply too absurd. No wonder she had had the impression Ransome was not telling her everything. She could little marvel that he had been averse to having her present herself at the front door as a potential lodger. He must have known very well what sort of house it was. The rogue, not to tell her!

Francie, realizing what a naive little fool he must think her, flushed hot, then cold with abject embarrassment. Images of hot tar and finger screws flashed in her mind, either one of which would have been too good for him. Even calling to mind every practical joke she or her sisters and brothers had ever played on one another, she could come up with nothing vile enough to suit the occasion. Egad, the least he could have done was be honest with her.

It was not until she looked up to see Philomene staring at her with an awed expression that Francie realized she must have been pacing up and down the room for several moments while she reviled Ransome's character, his probable fate, and his family heritage.

Francie came to an instant halt. It struck her forcibly that, in spite of wishing Ransome a dishonorable and ignominious end, it would little avail her to reveal that he was very probably somewhere in the house.

Instantly she bared her teeth in a grin, which must have looked as idiotic as it felt on her face.

"It's the room, of course," she said. "I'm afraid I was momentarily overwhelmed. Er—are they all like this?"

Philomene eyed her doubtfully. "Some bain't so nice. This were Flora's room," she said, as if that particular fact explained something which should have been obvious. Crossing to the wardrobe, Philomene ruffled through its contents, presumably in search of a dress.

Francie, in an attempt to order her thoughts in face of these new, unexpected developments, crossed with seeming aimlessness to the dressing table and picked up a crystal bottle. Pulling out the stopper, she sniffed experimentally at the liquid contents. "Who is Flora?" she asked, wrinkling her nose at the sweet whiff of attar of roses. Egad, she thought, rolling her eyes ceilingward, she might have known.

"She were Madame's best girl," Philomene confided, continuing without pause to search through the various garments hanging in the wardrobe, "till Flora crossed Madame. Flora ought never to have tried to run away. Madame don't hold with anyone going against her in that way. I never seen Madame so mad as when Ralph and Dinkerly Dan brung Flora back again. You being about her size, I expect this will do well enough." Pulling out a fantastic creation of pink feathers and fluff, she laid the gown across the bed. "You'd best put it on, miss," she added, looking at Francie with an expectant air. "Madame don't like to be kept waiting."

When it became obvious the girl did not intend to budge until she had seen Madame's orders carried out, Francie began reluctantly to undo the buttons of her dress.

"Won't Flora be needing that?" she asked hopefully, indicating the concoction in pink waiting in horrid significance on the bed.

"Not no more," said Philomene with utter certainty.

* * *

Harry drew back from the door that led to Madame Noire's sitting room. He had heard enough to know that Francie was on her way to one of the rooms where she would be dressed in the clothes of a Paphian. Bitterly he cursed the arrogance that had led him to believe Francie would be safe so long as she was with him. He had been a fool to leave her alone, even for a minute. But then, there was little point in dwelling on what he should have done. The question was what to do to get her back again.

Suddenly he tensed, his every sense alert. Almost immediately it came to him again—a muffled groan. He was sure of it. There was someone else in the room.

Following the low moans, Harry groped his way across the room to a second door. The water closet, no doubt, he speculated, reaching for the door handle. Locked, hell and the devil confound it. Who would put a lock on a bloody water closet?

Spurred by the groans, he fumbled for a penknife in the pocket of his greatcoat. At last, kneeling, he inserted the blade into the keyhole. At the click of the bolt sliding free, he smiled with grim satisfaction. No doubt he would have made an excellent living as a burglar, he congratulated himself, putting the knife away again. Now, my friend, he thought. Who the devil are you?

Harry thrust the door open—and was met with a crushing blow to the chest by a hurtling shoulder.

Harry staggered back, his arms wrapping instinctively about his assailant. He felt the body sag, a dead weight against him. Cursing silently, Harry lowered his burden to the floor of the closet.

Bloody hell. The poor devil was bound like a sheep for the slaughter. A gentleman of substance, thought Harry, from the quality of the fabric of the coat. Harry bit off a curse, as his hand came in contact with an ominous moist warmth over the left shoulder and chest. Harry was far too familiar with the heavy, sickening scent not to recognize it immediately for what it was. Whoever he was, the man was wounded and fast losing blood.

Deciding the circumstances warranted the risk, Harry tumbled for his tinderbox and a candle, which he found perched on a stool by the body.

Somehow he was only marginally surprised when Leighton's unmistakable features leaped up at him out of the gloom.

"The plot thickens, eh, my lord?" he murmured, checking the marquis's neck for a pulse. "You are alive at least, you bloody, damned fool, which is probably more than you deserve. Still, you are not lacking in nerve, I shall give you that."

Working swiftly, Harry quickly had Leighton free of his gag and rope manacles. A strip of petticoat, one presumably belonging to Madame Noire, served as a pad for the wound, while another was soon made into a bandage to hold the pad in place.

At last Harry, settling back on his heels, took time to consider his next move. He judged that little more than fifteen minutes had elapsed since Francie had been taken away—twenty at the most. Somehow he must contrive to move Leighton to a better place of safety, then locate the missing girl. He would tear the bloody place apart brick by brick, if need be, but he preferred to accomplish both missions without alerting Madame Noire to his presence.

Whatever Leighton was involved in, Harry had little doubt that it was better kept under wraps. Certainly the last thing any of them could wish was to have it come out that Lady Francine Powell and the Marquis of Leighton had been discovered under suspicious circumstances in a house of ill-repute and in, of all places, the notorious environs of Swallow Street.

It was readily apparent that there was only one safe avenue of escape for Leighton. He hoped the cursed drainpipe was sturdy enough for the weight of two grown men.

Francie, wryly surveying her image in the looking glass, could not but think it was a pity Lucy was not there to share this experience with her. She, at least, would have seen it as a remarkable opportunity to gather research.

Faith, if she had to dress up in a Paphian's finery, why did it have to be in pink? she reflected with a moue of disgust. She detested pink. Indeed, she did not doubt in the least that her predecessor had perished purely from an excess of it. Francie was sure that, rather than be forced to live in an environment of blushing rose, she would gladly have put a period to her own existence.

As for the gown itself, aside from its hideous color

and its profusion of feathers, it did lend a sort of provocative attraction, she decided, twisting her head over one shoulder to view it from the rear. Cut in a deep V in front and back, it left an inordinate amount of her back bare, not to mention her arms and shoulders and a wholly indecent expanse of her bosom. Furthermore, the slit up the front of the skirt seemed clearly designed to leave little to the imagination. Reaching an indecent height, it provided an unimpeded view not only of her ankles, but of her shins, her knees, and a goodly portion of her thighs, all encased in pink silk stockings held in place with lace garters embroidered in roses.

It came to her to wonder if Ransome would have found her in the least attractive in such a gown, only immediately to dismiss the notion as ridiculous in the extreme. Rather than find her appealing, he was far more likely to laugh. Her eyes flashed at the thought. But then, when she got through with him, very likely he would never laugh again.

She plopped down on the bed with a sigh. She would, that was, if she ever saw him again. Where the devil was he? she wondered, not for the first time since last she had seen him. He had been halfway up the drainpipe and she was on the point of starting after him, when the two overgrown apes had emerged from the carriage house and grabbed her from behind. It seemed like an eternity, but surely could not have been more than an hour since she had been presented to Madame Noire like a prize goose for the plucking. She did not believe for a moment that Ransome had abandoned her. The earl would never take the cow-

ard's way out. But what if he had been discovered and
rendered unconscious, or worse?

Damn Ransome, she fumed, aware of a knot at the
pit of her stomach. Why the deuce did he not come?
She would never forgive herself if something dreadful
had happened to him because of her.

She was just consigning him to the devil for causing
her what gave every manifestation of being an exquisite anguish, when she was startled to immediate attention by the turning of the doorhandle.

In an instant she was off the bed. Her heart ham-
mering, she hastily turned the lamp down to a feeble
glow. Then, snatching up a dainty pink parasol,
which was the closest thing to a weapon a thorough
search of the room had revealed to her, she took up
position behind and to one side of the door.

It was to come to her that Lily's male visitor must
be three sheets to the wind. Either that, or he was a
bumbling idiot. Why else, after all, should he seem
to be having no little difficulty turning the key in the
lock? She was heartily wishing her unseen caller to
the devil, when the click of the bolt sliding free
caused her heart to give a leap.

Francie grasped the parasol tightly in both hands
and raised it above her head. The doorhandle
turned, and the door started open. Francie caught
her breath. The shape of a man's head and shoulders
moved into her line of vision. Francie gritted her
teeth and tensed to bring the parasol crashing down.

"Francie—? The devil, are you in there?"

Francie let out an explosive breath.

"Ransome! Hell and the devil confound it." The

parasol toppled to the floor, and Francie flung herself against his tall, powerful frame. She would have beaten her fists against his chest had he not caught her wrists in both his hands and held her. "Where the *deuce* have you been? Have you any idea what I have been made to suffer, thinking you were lying dead or wounded someplace? What took you so long? Another few minutes and I should very likely have been made one of Madame Noire's permanent boarders."

Harry, judging with no small relief that Lady Powell was little harmed by her recent adventures, was next made aware of her interesting transformation.

"As eagerly as I am looking forward to a complete and unexpurgated account of your adventures," said Harry appreciatively as he released her in order to remove his greatcoat. "I'm afraid it must wait. In case you had forgotten, you, Lady Powell, have a masqued ball to attend."

"Oh, good God. Florence!" exclaimed Francie, who, in all the anticipation of being launched in a new career, had indeed let that particular slip her mind. "What time is it?"

"Well past midnight, I've no doubt." Harry held the greatcoat up. "Time enough, if we hurry."

Francie, however, had different ideas. Ignoring the greatcoat, she turned and paced a step, her mind weighing the possibilities. "Time enough, you mean, to search Madame Noire's private quarters." Wheeling about, she came back again. "Please, Ransome. I have it from a reliable source that she is presently out, and it is why we came, after all."

Harry, met with the pleading look that had more

than once been the instrument of his undoing, was moved to extreme measures.

"The truth is, Lady Powell," he said grimly, "that having just spent the last hour scaling a forty-foot drainpipe, not once, but twice, followed by an exceedingly uninspiring, not to mention perilous, tour of every room on the first two floors of Madame Noire's less than prestigious establishment, during which, I might add, I had the unfelicitous occasion to exchange words with not a few of her disgruntled patrons, I am in no mood to argue the point. I believe I have been more than patient. However, you will either put on this garment and accompany me to the carriage—now—or I shall be forced to drag you out in your present state of, shall we say, 'deshabille,' for want of a better word?"

Harry had the dubious satisfaction of seeing Francie's face go white, then red, with sudden, belated awareness of her unseemly appearance.

"Devil," she said, presenting her back to him. How dare he read *her* a curtain lecture. She was the one who had been forced to suffer the humiliation of stripping to the buff in order to be decked out in the paint and feathers of a Cyprian. Inserting her arms into the waiting coatsleeves with a great show of dignity, she turned once more to Ransome with a dangerous gleam in her eye. "I daresay, however, it is nothing you have not seen before."

"You may be sure of it, but never in so enticing a package," retorted Harry, in no mood to humor her impudence. "I believe, in fact, that I find a pink rose more pleasing to the eye than a white one. It is, after all, so much more colorful."

"Colorful! Egad, Ransome," exclaimed Francie in no little disgust. "Pink is perfectly dreadful. But not so dreadful as a boarding house that is in actuality a bordello. I may look and smell like a rose, but I am hardly a hothouse flower in danger of wilting. You could have warned me what to expect."

"No doubt, Lady Powell," Harry conceded grimly. "On the other hand, had you kept to the letter of our agreement instead of going off half-cocked on your own, you would have avoided a deal of unpleasantness and saved me no end of trouble."

"Half-cocked, did you say?" demanded Francie in tones of incredulity. "I wonder what you think I should have done when I saw two hulking brutes come out of the bushes at me? It seemed to me that it would little avail us if we were both discovered and taken. As a soldier, you should appreciate my diversionary tactics. You might at least have taken time to search Madame Noire's private quarters while you had the chance. Now, we shall only have it all to do over again."

"You are mistaken, Lady Powell," said Harry, taking Francie by the arm and impelling her out of the room and down the hall to the servants' stairs. "We are not going to return to this cursed house anytime in the near or distant future. Furthermore, if you ever put me through a moment even remotely resembling the one I experienced upon looking down from that cursed window to find you had utterly vanished, I shall most assuredly throttle you. Fortunately, a repeat performance of tonight's fiasco will not be necessary." Coming to the bottom of the stairs, he led her through a kitchen pantry and beyond, to a door, which was undoubtedly the service entrance. In another moment they were outside in what had once presumably been a garden, but which had long since given way to weeds and refuse. "As it happens," Harry added, making for the alleyway, "I stumbled onto something more important than any hypothetical documents."

Francie came to an abrupt halt. She was acutely aware of an immediate sinking sensation at something she sensed in Ransome's manner. Indeed, he did not have to tell her. She knew.

"Leighton," she gasped, feeling the blood drain from her face. "Good God, Ransome, say he is not dead."

"Softly, my girl," Harry said more gently than he had spoken to her yet. Feeling her sway against him, he grasped her firmly by the arms. "He has been hurt, but he is alive. He is in a place of safety, where even now he is receiving the care he needs."

Francie clutched at the lapels of Ransome's coat. "Where? Ransome, you must take me to him at once."

"On the contrary, you, Lady Powell, are going to Lady Desborough's masqued ball. No, *listen,* to me, Francie," Harry said forcefully, when Francie made as if to protest. "You will tell the marchioness that you are feeling ill and wish to return home immediately. By the time you arrive at Grosvenor Square, you will find the marquis is already there."

Francie tried to pull away. "But—"

"Think, my girl," Harry interrupted, giving her a shake. "You cannot want your sister to know where you have been tonight, let alone the circumstances under which we discovered her husband. Trust me to see the affair is wrapped in clean linen."

Francie was bewilderingly aware of Ransome's strength sustaining her own. Indeed, she could not imagine why she should find herself clinging to him as if she were no better than some silly female unable to think clearly. Naturally, he was in the right of it. Florence must never know about the house on Swallow Street.

Ashamed of herself, she resolutely straightened. "I do trust you. Indeed, you have been—" Whatever he had been, she was not allowed to finish. Her eyes widened as she glimpsed a hulking shape loom over them out of the darkness. A club-filled hand went up with obvious intent. "Good God, Ransome," she cried, shoving her hands against his chest with all her strength. "Behind you!"

Harry, blessed with quick reflexes, which had served to save his life on more than one occasion on the Continent, ducked, twisting around to meet his attacker. Launching himself beneath the descending club, he rammed his shoulder hard into the fellow's midriff. The brute staggered back, the wind knocked with a whoosh from his lungs. Harry, in no mood to prolong the engagement, drove his fist into the unprotected jaw.

It was over in a matter of seconds. Harry, winded from his exertions, drew in short breaths as, cursing, he shook the bleeding knuckles of his right hand.

Consequently, he was unaware of the second figure, barreling at him out of the shadows.

The missile, a loose cobblestone, plucked hastily from the carriage drive, sailed with unerring accuracy past Harry's ear to strike with a sickening thud in the center of Dinkerly Dan's massive forehead. The henchman, giving the appearance of one who had just encountered an impassable barrier, came to an abrupt halt, a peculiarly beatific expression on his brutish face. Then, like a tree trunk axed at the feet, he toppled backward to land with a resounding crash full-length on his back.

"So there," declared Francie, dusting her hands off with no little satisfaction. "Perhaps that will teach you to think twice the next time you feel the urge to man-handle a woman, you miserable excuse for a human being. That one, I daresay, was for Flora."

"Flora?" Ransome said, with the quizzical arch of an eyebrow.

Francie shook her head. "Never mind," she answered, tugging at his uninjured hand. "There isn't time. Suffice it to say that the two of them deserve far worse than they got."

"Worse?" Harry, pausing beside Dinkerly Dan's inert form, glanced appreciatively down at the fallen giant, who had a noticeable dent in his forehead. "One of your many boyish accomplishments, Lady Powell?" he queried, thinking it promised to be an interesting adventure in future to discover what other unique talents Lady Powell possessed.

Francie, feeling herself blush, could only be grateful for the concealing shadows. "As a matter of fact,

I have the dubious distinction of being able to knock
a bottle off a fence nine times out of ten at fifteen
yards. It is one of my more useful gifts, along with
being able to spit farther than either of my younger
brothers and to wrestle a full-grown sheep to the
ground for shearing. I have been a sad trial, I fear,
to my mama, who is in every respect a lady of refined
sensibilities."

Harry, who was fast gaining a greater appreciation
of precisely the sort of mama Lady Bancroft must
have been to rear such an offspring, smiled faintly to
himself. "Judging from her daughter, I should say
she must be a remarkable parent."

"Having successfully brought up seven children,
she is truly a paragon of patience and understanding.
I have no doubt you would like her exceedingly well."

A low whicker alerted Francie to the fact that the
spavined gelding along with the weathered hackney
had apparently failed to inspire avarice in the hearts
of any passerby. They were both still waiting in the
vacant lot—along, it would seem, with a newly ac-
quired and diminutive tiger.

"You took long enough, m'lord," observed that
personage in a voice that was hardly that of a child.
Climbing down the wheel of the hackney, he dropped
to the ground. "I was beginning to think you might
be in need of reinforcements, but I see you found
your lady well enough. Did you meet with trouble?"

"Only a small encounter with Madame Noire's two
bodyguards. Nothing, it would seem, that the lady
could not have handled herself. This, in case you are
wondering," Harry added, turning to Francie, "is an

old acquaintance who has agreed to help us. He has, in fact, been of service to me on more than one occasion since our chance meeting some years ago."

"The occasion of me trying to hold him up one night, m'lady," laughed the little man, baring his head to reveal in the moonlight a not unhandsome face framed in curly red hair. "His lordship's a right 'un, he is. Took it all in the proper spirit. Not like some I could name was I of a mind to."

"My old friend, you will be interested to know," Ransome supplied with dancing eyes, "is in the business of designing gowns for some of the finest modistes in Bond Street. It seems he is considered a positive genius. He has promised to drive you to Lady Desborough's ball, while I see to Leighton. Lady Francine, allow me to present . . ."

"Laughing Jack Cates," Francie finished for Ransome in astonished accents. "I could not be more pleased to make your acquaintance, sir."

The masqued ball at Lady Desborough's was still in full swing when Francie, having hastily donned her Egyptian robes and veil, made her entrance by the back way. She could not but be grateful the affair was a shocking squeeze. In the crush of people, she felt reasonably confident that her absence had not been noted.

In this she was soon to discover she had been greatly mistaken. Hardly had she made her appearance in the ballroom by way of the terrace than she was confronted by an almost identical version of herself.

"So," declared Francie's double, dragging Francie forcibly into an alcove fronted by a potted palm. "You decided to come back after all."

"Flo," Francie exclaimed, clasping her sister's hand in both her own. "Thank heavens. I was—"

"Pray do not 'Flo' me," Florence interrupted, obviously in a high dudgeon. "Did you think I was such a slow top as not to realize when I have been made the dupe? Not that it was not very clever of you to insist we dress alike. You may be sure it worked like a charm. Whenever I inquired if someone had seen you, I was informed that you were in the ballroom or on the terrace or most definitely in the supper room. I pursued that vanishing phantom for nearly an hour before I realized it was myself I was chasing. Where the devil have you been, Francine Elizabeth Powell? And pray do not tell me one of your Banbury stories. You are perilously close to finding yourself on your way back to Greensward."

Francie, realizing she was fairly caught, experienced a sudden and immediate sense of relief. It was the one thing in Ransome's plan that had occasioned her no little discomfort—she had not liked the idea of lying to Florence. It was time, after all, that her sister and brother-in-law did away with all the silly secrets and had a heart-to-heart talk with one another.

"But I have no intention of feeding you a falsehood," Francie hastened to assure Florence. "In fact, I was just coming to find you to tell you everything. But not here, Flo. Bear with me just a little while longer. I shall tell you what you wish to know in the carriage."

"Francie, for heaven's sake," Florence said, her beautiful eyes above the veil darkening with trepidation. "You are frightening me. What is it? What have you done?"

"Nothing. Or at least nothing that will not be made plain to you in a very few moments. As it happens, I have had the most bizarre adventure in which figured two behemoths by the name of Ralph and Dinkerly Dan, a fallen woman called Flora, and the most delightful highwayman called Laughing Jack." Squeezing her sister's hand, Francie drew her out of the alcove. "Come. We shall take our leave of Lady Desborough and summon the carriage. It is time we were going home."

Eleven

Francie, sitting curled up in a chair at Leighton's bedside, let her thoughts wander as she listened to the rain spattering against the windowpane. It was well past midnight of the fourth night since the marquis had been brought home more dead than alive from what had proved to be a knife wound high up on the left side of his chest near the shoulder. Weakened from loss of blood and stricken with fever, he had wavered between delirium and fretful sleep until early that morning when at last the fever had broken.

Florence, who had refused to leave Leighton's bedside for that first interminable night and all the next day, when Paul had sunk so low, had at last been ordered from the sickroom by Dr. Evans, who declared her ladyship would be of little use to anyone, and least of all to Leighton, if she became a patient herself. As Florence would not hear of hiring a stranger to sit with Leighton, Flo had at last been prevailed upon to allow Francie to share the sickroom duties. They were ably assisted in their endeavors by Osgood Gilcrest, Leighton's personal servant, who maintained a calm demeanor even in the face of Leighton's worst throes of delirium, and by Ransome, who, though he did not help in the sickroom, had proven to be a tower of strength in all other respects.

A daily caller, Ransome had made sure Francie was out of the house every afternoon, if only for a few minutes' walk in the garden. It was he who spread it about that Leighton had suffered an injury in a carriage accident, he who sent word to the Earl and Countess of Bancroft of their son-in-law's mishap, he who took care of all the endless details of warding off the inquisitive.

Francie, who had all she could do to keep Florence's spirits up and to help with the nursing, was hardly aware of all that he did on their behalf. She knew only that it was as though an invisible shield had been erected to protect her and her loved ones from the rest of the world.

No doubt she would have been astounded to discover that Ransome's impregnable guard went so far as to include armed men posted about the house on Grosvenor Square, and with good reason.

Veronique Noire, having failed to return to Swallow Street in the wake of Leighton's escape and Francie's introduction to the seamier aspects of Madame's boarding house for itinerant actresses, was nowhere to be found. Not even Laughing Jack Cates's extensive network of street urchins, prostitutes, and panhandlers had been able to uncover a clue as to her whereabouts. It seemed that, until Leighton regained his senses and was able to clear up certain matters, Madame Noire would have to wait.

In the meantime, Harry meant to make sure the

inhabitants of the house on Grosvenor Square were safe from the woman's evil machinations. A further attempt against Leighton's life was hardly inconceivable, and should Lily's real identity become known to Madame Noire, Francie herself would be in danger. Fortunately, Francie's ball had had to be indefinitely postponed and her activities suspended, a circumstance which Harry could only view with relief. It was far simpler to protect her if she was out of circulation. Madame Noire, after all, had seen Francie in all her guises. As unlikely as it was that the actress would find herself in the same vicinity as Francie, it was not an impossibility. Harry had little doubt in such a case that the woman would recognize Francie at once.

What Harry could not know was that Francie had come to the same conclusion herself. It had, in fact, just occurred to her that the best way to bring Madame Noire out into the open was to set herself up as bait for a trap, when she became aware that Leighton had opened his eyes and was looking at her with every appearance of lucidity.

"Paul," she exclaimed softly, laying her hand against the side of his face. "Thank God. We have been so worried. How are you feeling?"

Leighton swallowed and licked dry lips. "Weak . . . as an . . . infant. Have been dreaming. Strange dreams. I remember—" He stopped, a frown etching itself between his eyebrows. "How did I—?"

"Never mind that for now," Francie said hastily, reaching for a glass of water by the bedside. "You are here and you are safe." Lifting his head, she held the glass to his lips until he had managed to swallow a few sips. "There. You must lie quiet now while I fetch Flo. She has been beside herself with worry. I have after a deal of persuasion prevailed upon her to rest."

"No." Leighton's fingers closed weakly about Francie's wrist. "Don't disturb her."

"I wish you will not be absurd. She has been in constant attendance at your side. She would never forgive me if I did not let her know at once you are back with us again." Gently pulling free of his grasp, she smiled. "Besides, we must get some broth down you—now you are awake."

Francie crossed to the door that joined Leighton's room with Florence's.

"You have been very ill, Paul, and you are not out of the briars yet, but the fever has broken, and Dr. Evans assures us you are past the worst of it. Now, I shall just go and bring Flo to you. Promise you will remain quiet."

Before he could voice the protest that was clearly on his lips, Francie slipped into the other room where her sister lay, fully dressed, across the bed.

"Flo," she murmured softly, giving her sister a small shake. "Flo, dear, wake up."

Florence bolted awake, her eyes wide with alarm. "Francie? What is it? Is Paul—"

"Yes, it is Paul. He is awake, Flo, and waiting to see you."

In an instant Florence was off the bed and across the room. Francie, following, came to the door in time to see Florence fling herself down on her knees beside the bed.

"Paul, my darling, you are awake at last." Weeping and smiling, she clasped his hand to her lips. "My dearest love, I have been so frightened for you, but now you will begin to get well. You are here with me, and that is all that matters. Everything is going to be all right, I know it."

Tears started in Francie's eyes as Leighton's voice little stronger than a whisper, carried to her. "Florence, my dear child. I believe you really mean that."

"But of course I mean it. And I am not a child. I am a woman who has been in torment. Paul, whatever I have done to alienate your affections, pray say that it is not too late for me to make up for it. I swear I shall die if—if you cannot love me."

"Cannot love you?" Leighton's answer, couched in accents of amazement, came stronger then. "My God, I could never stop loving you, even when you made it clear to me you married me only for my fortune and my title, and I swore I should never trouble you again with my presence. I could not bear the thought that you would make love to me out of duty."

"But why—*how* could you have conceived such a notion? On our honeymoon, I thought . . . Faith, was I so—so very dreadful?"

"You were everything that I had hoped and more. It was what you said to your sister Lucy the day we arrived home. I had stepped out on the terrace to have a cigar. You never knew I was there. I heard you say . . ."

"Oh, my God, I remember. I boasted to Lucy that you were both titled and wealthy, everything I had ever looked for in a husband. That you were also young, handsome, and seemingly head over ears in love with me was like icing on the cake. It was true, Paul. I was a vain, foolish woman. I—I did not know then what I know now, what I learned to my bitter torment all those dreadful weeks when I thought I had lost you. I love you, Paul, with my whole heart, my entire being. I have from the very beginning. Without you, nothing matters. If I cannot have you, my life will be utterly without meaning."

Francie, drawing quietly away, yet witnessed enough of Leighton's answer, couched in a sudden, long embrace, to be certain that Florence's future promised to be everything one might have expected for the acknowledged Beauty of the family.

Smiling to herself, Francie sent word to the kitchens to have broth taken up to his lordship. Then, judging that her presence would not be required in the sickroom for some time, she wandered downstairs to the study with the vague notion of dashing a letter off to her mama and papa with the happy news.

She was suffused with a warm glow of happiness for Paul and her sister, which was accompanied by a peculiar hollow sensation. She tried to tell herself it was only inevitable that she should experience a certain let-down after the passing of a crisis and that it certainly had nothing to do with the fact that she was just a trifle envious of her sister's happiness. As hard as she tried, however, she could not quite dispel the troublesome fancy that she would have liked it very well if a certain nobleman with piercing blue eyes and a smile that had the power to turn her knees to jelly would love her, if only a little.

She, after all, had irrevocably and irretrievably lost her heart to him no little time ago.

It really was not in the least fair that she should have fallen head over ears for a man noted for the beautiful women he kept. If she had to fall for someone, it might at least have been for someone who was not so far above her touch. It was not that she thought of herself as an antidote, she reflected practicably. She knew she was possessed of at least passable looks. Looks, however, would avail her nothing if the man in question persisted in seeing her as a kid of a girl who, engaging though she might be, had nevertheless caused him no end of trouble. He had, after all, seen nearly all there was to see of her without really seeing her at all!

No, she told herself as she came to the study door. Clearly she must reconcile herself to the fact that Ransome very likely would be glad enough to see the last of her now that Leighton was safely home and hardly likely to fall a second time to the lures of Madame Noire or anyone else, for that matter, other than his adoring young wife.

With a moue of disgust, she opened the study door and stepped in—to be immediately blasted by a gust of wind-driven rain. She saw at a glance that the French windows were standing agape, apparently blown open in the fury of the storm.

Slamming the door closed behind her, she hastened across the room. A brief but fierce struggle to shut out the storm left her wet and shivering with cold.

The devil, she thought, shaking out her sodden skirts as she turned.

The sudden blow came out of nowhere. Francie's head shot back, and myriad lights exploded in her brain. The next instant the floor rushed up to meet her.

She must have lost consciousness for a moment or two; indeed, she had the oddest sensation of rising slowly out of the depths of a dark abyss to an awareness of voices clashing over her.

"What do you mean you know her?" demanded a masculine voice in tones of incredulity. Armstead, thought Francie hazily, unable to find the will to open her eyes. "She is the marchioness, one must presume."

"She is the girl Lily, I tell you. The one who came to my house that night with a preposterous story about needing a room. If you had come that night as you promised, you would know. If you had kept your word, we would not now be in the fix we are in."

"And if you had finished the job the way you should have done, Leighton would now be dead, and there would be no need to clean up your mess for you. As for the girl, it would seem the marchioness is an enterprising female. I daresay she was desirous of learning something about her husband's mistress. Curious, from what I had heard of her, she hardly seemed the sort to dare such a perilous stunt."

"She had help," Madame Noire reminded him. "The man who took her from my house was undoubtedly the Earl of Ransome. There could be no mistaking Ralph's description. I have every reason to believe, my dear Armstead, you are in the presence of Ransome's mysterious White Rose. It is *tres amusant, n'est ce pas?*"

"I should say it is a pity her ladyship did not stick with her sewing and knitting. Obviously, she cannot be allowed to live. She knows far too much. On the other hand, she can wait. The documents are our first priority. Our mutual benefactor is not the sort to view failure with any tolerance. Nor is he a patient man. I suggest it behooves us to find the cursed papers before he returns from finishing off Leighton. I daresay his lordship has a wall safe somewhere. Check the paintings. I shall examine the bookshelves."

Francie, who was suffering a swift stab of horror at the realization that there was someone else in the house, a cold-blooded murderer who had every intention of cutting Leighton's stick for him, went stiff at the sound of the door being thrust open.

"I'm afraid you are wasting your time, Armstead," announced Ransome in chilling accents, which Francie, nearly collapsing with relief, could not but find exceedingly welcome. "The documents you are after never left the Lords of Admiralty. I believe I must ask you for the pistol in your coat pocket. As for you, madam, I have it from a reliable source that you are never without a knife. You will kindly hand it over to my friend, here."

The room had fallen into a sudden, tense silence, which was dispelled by a low hiss from Madame Noire.

"*Sacriste,* it is you," she said in venomous accents. "I had happily thought you dead long ago."

"Tsk, tsk, Veronique. Is that any way to greet an old friend? You were not so high and mighty when you were one of the Scarlet Women of Swallow Street," observed a sardonic voice, which Francie could not but immediately recognize. "And after I provided you the means of setting yourself up in business. I daresay you fancy yourself above your old associates since you started hobnobbing with the gentry."

"I say, Ransome," interjected Armstead in tones of grim amusement. "Your acquaintanceship is not lacking in originality. First, the intriguing White Rose, and now Laughing Jack Cates, one must presume."

"At your service, gov'nor. And now that gun, if you please."

Francie, feeling someone kneel beside her, struggled to sit up, only to have strong hands gently, but firmly push her down again.

"Softly, my girl," said Harry, his stern features exceedingly grim at sight of the dark purplish bruise that marred the purity of Francie's skin on the left side of her jaw. "The devil, Francie. Are you hurt?"

"No, no. Only a trifle stunned." Francie clutched at Harry's coat lapels with frantic hands. "Ransome, upstairs. Hurry. There is another intruder after Leighton."

"Gently, child." Harry, an arm beneath her knees and her shoulders, carefully lifted Francie and carried her to the sofa. Laying her down, he knelt beside her. "Leighton and your sister are perfectly safe, I assure you. I have already seen to the gentleman in question."

"You have?" Francie, who had been clinging to Harry, pulled a little away in order to gaze in wonder up at him. "But how did you know? Indeed, how is it that you are here at all?"

"How not, when I have been here every night since we brought Leighton home?"

"Here?" Francie's face lit with undisguised delight at his cleverness. "But, how delectably scandalous. Where in the house, Ransome?"

"In the room across from yours, which is how I was able to intercept your upstairs intruder before he could do any harm. A pity he managed to escape before I could see his face. Still, Jack was able to spot these two in time to stop me from leaving in pursuit. He, you will be interested to know, has been posted outside with numerous of his—er—business associates."

"Have you, Jack?" Francie smiled, gazing past Ransome at the little man, who had just finished binding his two prisoners with a length of drapery cord.

"It was my pleasure, m'lady," Jack grinned back at her. "Couldn't have Veronique, here, causing any more trouble. My responsibility. I set her up in business, you see."

"Thank you, Jack. I am very much obliged to you. And to you, Ransome." Feeling suddenly immeasurably weary, Francie sighed and laid her head back against the arm of the couch. "Really, my lord, I fear I am becoming a sad trial to you," she said, assaying a wan smile. "I am exceedingly grateful, however, that you have come to rescue me yet again. I wonder, would you be so kind as to help me up? Somehow, I cannot seem to stop the room from spinning."

"You, my girl, are going to remain where you are while I send for the doctor," Harry answered, thinking hanging would be too good for the man who had used his fist on her. A signet ring complete with the family crest had left its unmistakable mark on her skin. "Keep an eye on those two, Jack," he added, coming to his feet. "Shoot them if they so much as make a move."

Francie, chilled at something she sensed in his manner, reached a hand out to Ransome. "Don't go, Ransome, I beg you. Truly, I am all right. Send Jack if you must insist on a doctor."

As Ransome, however, was already well on his way, this last was uttered to the accompaniment of the door slamming shut behind him.

Taking the stairs two at a time, Harry soon came to the room he had occupied the past several days. There, he paused only long enough to retrieve the sword that instinct or foresight, perhaps, had prompted him to bring with him.

Harry arrived at No. Ten Berkeley Square as dawn was breaking behind a grey ceiling of clouds. Finding the door conveniently ajar, as though someone had hurriedly entered only moments before him, he let himself in without bothering to knock. With long, sure strides, he made his way through the darkened halls to a closed door.

Knowing what he would find on the other side, he flung the door open.

"Laverly!" he called out in ringing accents.

"Ah, Harry," observed the figure seated in the glow of a single lamp, which cast shadows over the spacious confines of a study. "I wondered how long it would take you to arrive. As it happens, you are just in time for a drink. My last, as it were, unless fortune is kinder than I have been led to expect it to be. It was devilish bad luck that I should have found the Earl of Ransome waiting for me tonight. I do not suppose you would care to enlighten me, old friend, as to how you came to be at Leighton's? I was not aware you were on intimate terms with the marquis."

Harry, who, having flung off his greatcoat, was in the process of removing his coat, shrugged with cold indifference. "No, how could you, 'old friend'? I hardly know the marquis. It was pure chance that led me to fall victim to love at this particular moment in time. As it happens I have every expectation of marrying the marquis's sister-in-law."

"His sister-in-law. Good God," exclaimed Laverly, staring, thunderstricken, at Harry. "So that is why you made your singular appearance at Almack's. I heard the rumors, but I placed no credence in them. After all, I saw you with the White Rose. *She* was clearly more in your style, Harry, than a country miss straight out of the schoolroom."

"Fortunately, this country miss happens to be a woman of many facets. It is not given to every man to meet a female who can incorporate the allurement and mystery of the White Rose with the unpredictability and liveliness of youth and innocence. She has a propensity for irresistible impulse, did you know? I shall never be bored with her as my wife. But then, that should hardly be news to you, Edward. I believe you know, the lady," Harry murmured in steely accents. "You ran into her, if I am not mistaken, at the Pork Pie Inn in Melton Mowbray. Or perhaps it would be more accurate to say you ran in pursuit of her."

Laverly's handsome lips curved in sudden understanding. "Ah, the eavesdropper on the terrace. I believe I begin to see, Harry. Is that where you met her? After you left Lady Catherine at the hunting lodge? Ironic, is it not? I should have given anything for the sort of tryst with the beautiful green-eyed temptress that you so casually tossed away. I *have* given everything in a vain pursuit of her. Regrettably, Lady Catherine's tastes are damnably expensive, and my resources, I fear, are not what they once were. I have never had your luck with either the cards or the ladies."

"You are mistaken, Edward," Harry replied, significantly removing first one boot then the other. "It is not luck, but knowing the cards. Lady Catherine has always been a losing proposition. She is incapable of loving anyone, but herself."

"Yes, there is always that," murmured Laverly, staring, unseeing, into the amber liquid in his glass. "Still, I should have gone on loving her if only out of the vain hope that one day she might actually see me as a man. I daresay you could never understand why I should lend myself to blackmail and treason for the sake of a woman."

"The truth is I do not care why you should have done it," Harry said with chilling directness. "I am not here because you employed Armstead and Madame Noire to compromise men of influence in order to gain state secrets. For that, I should gladly have left you to the hangman. Your mistake was in leaving your mark on my future wife. You should not have struck her, Edward. I might never have known it was you, had you not left the imprint of your signet ring on her skin." Ransome drew the sword from its scabbard. "For that cowardly assault and because you meant to murder her and the others, I shall most assuredly put a period to your existence."

Laverly appeared to wince at Ransome's pronouncement of judgment, accompanied by the cold ring of steel.

Deliberately, he raised the glass to his lips.

"Are you sure you will not have a drink, Harry? This is a particularly fine French brandy. No? Ah, well." Tossing his head back, he drained the glass. "A pity to waste it, but what would you? It seems we have more pressing matters to attend."

Setting the glass on the desk before him, he bent down with the apparent intention of removing his boots.

"I am sorry about the girl, Harry," Laverly said. "I should not have liked cutting her stick for her, anymore than I enjoyed striking her with my fist. You do understand I was left little choice in the matter, do you not? Just as *you* leave me little choice, old friend."

Straightening, he came to his feet, a small, but deadly looking pistol, held in his hand.

"I really dislike the notion of dying, you see," he said, coming around the edge of the desk, "and I have, after all, witnessed what you can do with a sword. I'm afraid, old son, that you are about to be shot for a burglar. Naturally, I shall be devastated by my tragic error."

"Naturally," Harry responded dryly. Holding the point of the sword lightly between the thumb and forefinger of his left hand, he smiled coldly. "Not even a last shred of honor, Edward? You disappoint me. But then, I was a fool to expect more from a panderer. It would seem Lady Catherine has better judgment than that for which I gave her credit. A man who is a coward may be pitied. One without honor is less than a man."

Laverly visibly paled with anger.

"Damn you, Harry," he said. "You never did mince words. I believe I shall enjoy killing you, after all."

Harry's lip curled mockingly. "Are you sure, Edward? It is one thing to kill in the heat of battle, but quite another to gun a man down in cold blood while he is looking you in the eyes. Perhaps you would like me to turn my back."

Laverly took a step forward, the gun extended. "Damn you, stop! Don't move, I tell you."

Harry lunged to one side. Laverly fired. Ransome's sword arm flashed forward, then back. The viscount went suddenly still. His face twisted in terrible realization as he stared down at the red stain spreading across the white fabric of his shirt. Slowly, he dropped to his knees.

"Bloody hell, Harry," he gasped, lifting his eyes to Ransome's. "Never . . . could . . . beat you at . . . anything."

With a long sigh, he fell forward at Ransome's feet.

Twelve

"Francie, you cannot leave us now," declared Florence, regarding her sister in no little exasperation. "I won't let you. The Season is not over yet, and there is your ball to reschedule now that Paul is mending. I simply will not hear of your going."

"I'm afraid there is nothing you can do to stop me," Francie replied, as she oversaw Daisy in the packing of her trunks. "And, really, I wish you will not try. I have had enough of London and the Season to last a lifetime. I want to go home, Flo, to Greensward."

"But why?" Florence plopped down on the bed. "Greensward will still be there a fortnight from now. Why must you fling all away, just when everything is going so splendidly? I daresay in another two weeks Paul will be strong enough for us to go with you. And there is Ransome. He loves you, Francie. Surely you must know that. Why else, after all, would he have fought a duel with Laverly over you. He might just as easily have turned the viscount over to the Bow Street Runners as risked his life in a sword fight."

"But that's just it. He swore he would not fight for me. He gave me his word. And what did he do the moment my back was turned, but go and challenge Laverly to a duel. You must see how utterly impossible that makes everything. I am prone to cataclysmic misadventure, Flo, you know I am. I cannot seem to help myself. And I will not have Ransome risking his life to save mine every time I find myself in hot water. At least at Greensward, I am not like to endanger anyone but myself."

Florence, who had spent the past thirty minutes talking herself blue in the face, was as close as she had ever been to losing all patience with Francie. "Good heavens. Of all the muddleheaded excuses I have ever heard, that one is the lamest. Laverly was a traitor. He deserved what Harry gave him. From what Harry said, I daresay Laverly welcomed it. He saved the viscount from the scandal of a hangman's noose. Surely you must see that. The viscount was head of a ring of spies who used Madame Noire's establishment to extort influential men for state secrets. It was why Paul went undercover—to ferret Laverly out. The man betrayed his country for money, and all because of his obsession with a spoiled, greedy woman who could not love him. Lady Catherine is as much to blame as anyone."

"Perhaps, but it little signifies. The truth is, I have not heard a word from Ransome for over a se'ennight, which is indication enough that you are wholly mistaken in your analysis. If he loved me, do you think he would have taken himself off someplace as soon as he was certain the danger here was past? You might as well accept the fact that he is a man of nobility and generosity who would have done for any female in

trouble precisely what he did for me. It does not mean
that he entertains any great feelings of affection for
me. On the contrary, I daresay he is glad to be rid of
me. And who could blame him? I have been nothing
but a thorn in his side since I thrust myself in his
arms."

Francie's voice, to her disgust, broke most reveal-
ingly on that final utterance. Stifling a gasp, she
turned her back on Flo. "And now I believe I must
ask you to excuse me, Florence. I have a great deal
of packing to do if I am to be away before noon."

Florence, flinging up her hands, got up and walked
to the door. "Oh, indeed. Pray do not let me keep
you from it. I daresay you will be very happy playing
auntie the rest of your life to all your nieces and
nephews. Indeed, the role of eccentric spinster will
undoubtedly suit you perfectly well."

Closing the door and leaning for a moment with
her back to it, Florence smiled to herself. She might
have failed to make the least impression on her sister,
but she had learned what she had set out to discover.
Francie was head over ears in love with Ransome, and
that was all she needed to know.

Pushing away from the door, she made straight to
her sitting room and, seating herself at her secretary,
pulled out a leaf of writing paper. Quill in hand, she
paused for one last struggle with her conscience. She
could not be mistaken in Francie's feelings for Ransome. The girl loved him. But what if she were wrong
about Harry? She had only come to know the earl
those few days when Paul had lain so dreadfully ill,
and yet she had come with surprising ease to trust in

him, even to like him. He might indeed be a rake,
but he was also a man, a very fine man to whom she
would not hesitate to entrust her sister's happiness
and well-being, and that was all that really mattered.
Francie had been instrumental in saving Florence's
home, her marriage, her husband, indeed, her love.
It was only right that Flo should do the same for her
sister, even if it meant betraying that sister's trust.

Pulling the leaf of paper to her, Florence began to
write.

Francie, for once in her life, did not find herself
fretting at being cooped up in a carriage or reflecting
that, had she been a boy, she might have been driving
her own curricle and pair through the fabulous
Quorn country. If nothing else, she had come in the
past month and a half, not to mention the last three
days on the road, to realize that she was inescapably
a female, one prone, moreover, to all the foibles peculiar to her sex.

Suffering the miseries of unrequited love and sunk
in a slough of despondency, however, she could find
little to recommend in the feminine condition.

Still, she supposed there must be some compensa-
tion for feeling as if one had been kicked in the stomach by a horse. She could not deny, after all, that Lucy
had been right when she predicted Francie's sojourn
in London would be a grand, glorious adventure. She
doubted there were many girls who could lay claim to
the distinction of having been the most talked about
woman in London, let alone having been abducted

into a brothel or helped to bring a traitor to justice. And, in truth, she would not have traded these adventures for diamonds or gold. They were the most glorious moments of her entire life, and she owed them all to Harry Danvers, the Earl of Ransome.

In future, no doubt she would derive a nostalgic benefit from dragging them up again for retrospection. For now, however, they occasioned her a bittersweet ache in the vicinity of her breastbone. And that, too, she reflected dourly, she owed to Harry Danvers.

It had occurred to her more than once that last week of waiting for a light, thrilling footstep to cross her threshold, that Ransome might at least have come to say good-bye before he decided to seemingly vanish off the face of the earth. Certainly there was nothing to keep him from it. Thanks to Leighton, the earl had not had to face charges for duelling. If anything, he had won the gratitude of his government. The entire matter had been viewed by the Lords of Admiralty as a tidy end to what promised to be a nasty scandal.

No, Francie reflected, staring out the window at the undulating wolds and green sheep pastures embraced by narrow lanes and high hedges. She very much feared there could only be one explanation for Ransome's disappearance. It would be, after all, the simplest manner in which to sever ties that had undoubtedly become exceedingly tiresome. When one went to the heart of the matter, she could hardly blame him for taking the easy way out.

* * *

The inn on the outskirts of Crowle was just as she remembered it, even to the curricle and pair in the yard attended by a yawning tiger in blue livery. Daisy, who had apparently overcome her tendency to motion sickness by having frequent recourse to a posset supplied her by Laughing Jack Cates with whom she had, unbeknownst to Francie, struck up a friendship during his sojourn outside the house on Grosvenor Square, happily alit from the coach unaided by Francie.

"Well, here we be, m'lady, less than a day's drive from Greensward," she said, shaking out her skirts. "I daresay you will be feeling more the thing once you lay eyes on the moors again."

"Yes, no doubt," replied Francie, wishing her lady's maid could manage to be a trifle less cheerful. The abigail had seemed positively to radiate good spirits the entire miserable three days in the coach, so much so, in fact, that Francie had come to suspect Daisy might very well be three sheets to the wind. "Certainly, I shall be glad to be quit of the coach."

Francie, leading the way into the inn, could not but reflect that, under different circumstances, she would undoubtedly have looked forward to a hot bath and the hearty fare for which the inn was noted. She had always fancied she would enjoy junketing about the world. That was before a gimlet-eyed nobleman had disrupted the even tenor of her life, however, and caused her to forever put her youth behind her. No doubt Florence was in the right of it, and she would soon become accustomed to a future spent as a spinster upon the shelf, she told herself—and she was not in the least comforted by the thought.

"Look, m'lady," Daisy whispered as they entered the common room, "there be an old friend of yours."

Francie, glancing where Daisy was looking, experienced an immediate sinking sensation. "Good heavens. Sir Fancy-Lace. It needed only that. I daresay if we ignore him, he will not bother us."

Hardly had she come to that assessment of the situation than the squire, resplendent in a crimson Jean de Bry coat with unconscionably high shoulder pads and canary yellow cossacks with ribbons around the ankles, lifted his eyes to hers.

In the moment of instantaneous recognition following the meeting of glances, Sir Fancy-Lace gave expression to a fierce grimace of unmitigated dislike.

"It's a fine thing when a man is no longer free to enjoy a pint in his favorite inn without having his peace and tranquillity disturbed by females," he observed sourly. "Shouldn't you be somewhere writing out invitations for your wedding, my lady, or having your gown made up at the very least?"

Francie, in no mood to indulge in repartee, gay or otherwise, with the gentleman, parted her lips to inform him that he need not concern himself. She had no intention of cutting up his peace and quiet. Far from it, she wished only for her supper and her bed.

She was prevented, however, from delivering that reassuring speech by the intervention of a cool, masculine drawl issuing from behind her.

"As a matter of fact, that is precisely where she should be."

Francie, sustaining a wild shock of joy, spun around.

The tall figure of the earl stood just inside the door, a greatcoat flowing from his shoulders. His eyes burned with a steely light. His hair, usually fashionably dishevelled, fell over his forehead in disarray. Dust and lines of fatigue marked the stern features. Faith, he had never looked so formidable.

"Ransome?" she exclaimed, suddenly uncertain.

Harry held her with his unwavering stare. "Unfortunately, the lady is impetuous, headstrong, and impossibly stubborn. She absolutely refuses to believe she could be the object of a man's serious intentions. Which is why you leave me no choice, my dear, but to resort to extreme measures."

With a single, long stride, Ransome closed the intervening distance between them. Without warning, he bent down and, catching Francie behind the knees, slung her over his shoulder before she could do more than utter a gasp of startled outrage and surprise.

"Inform your employer that, having been driven beyond the bounds of endurance by his impossible daughter, I have at last taken matters into my own hands," said Harry to Daisy, who was grinning with undisguised glee. "If he wishes to express an objection, he may find us on the road to Gretna Green."

"Good God, Ransome," Francie exclaimed in horror. "Are you mad? You cannot send such a message to my father."

"I not only can, my dear, but I just have," grimly replied Harry, carrying her out of the inn. "And if I have lost my reason, there is no one to blame for it but yourself. No one could expect a man to remain rational in the face of all that I have been made to endure for the sake of an impossibly obstinate female with a predilection for impulsive behavior which has led her to parade herself in the most provocative manner possible as my mistress while denying that I could possibly be attracted to her. For the sake of delicacy, I shall not even mention a particularly revealing incident in a house that was never a haven for itinerant actresses.''

"Oh! I might have known you would fling that in my face!'' declared Francie, greatly incensed.

"Indeed you might,'' retorted Harry, depositing her without ceremony on the seat of his curricle. Climbing up beside her, he spread a rug over her lap, then took up the reins and the whip. "That singularly memorable event has, after all, served to keep me awake at nights. I shall probably bring it up on numerous occasions in future—whenever I deem it advisable to remind you that I am not entirely impervious to your womanly attributes.''

Lifting the reins, he set the team in motion at a splitting pace.

Francie, forced to clutch at the siderail to keep from being flung out by the lurch of the curricle, thought indeed he must be mad. Even with the light of a full moon, they were traveling at a dangerous clip. Still, she could not but thrill at the ease with which Ransome handled his cattle. Even in the absence of rationale, he would appear to have the situation well in hand.

Still, it behooved her to save him from his folly. No

doubt he was right to blame her for his present state of insanity. Her mama had said she would drive a saint to drink.

Relaxing by degrees, Francie studied the stern profile from beneath the veil of her eyelashes.

Taken unawares at the inn, she had not had time to consider things in a rational manner. Perhaps it was not too late to bring him to his senses. He was, after all, a man of logic.

"I beg you, my lord, to reconsider your actions," she ventured carefully, lest she upset his delicate balance. "You cannot truly mean to take me to Gretna Green. I daresay you have not thought the matter through."

Harry smiled exceedingly grimly. "I am well aware of the light in which you view my mental capacities, Lady Powell. I have, after all, been at great pains to disabuse you of the notion that I am a mindless paragon of virtue who could not possibly be motivated by more primitive urges. That I have failed utterly in that endeavor is precisely why we find ourselves on our present course. The truth is, Lady Powell, that I am determined that you will be my wife. I believe I cannot make it any plainer than that."

"Now you are being utterly absurd, Ransome," Francie informed him in reasonable tones. "You know very well you do not have the least desire to marry me. I cannot hold a candle to Lady Catherine, or any of your other barques of frailty for that matter. Why, you yourself have taken any number of occasions to point out that I have caused you no end of trouble. And you are perfectly in the right of it. I am stubborn, headstrong, and hopelessly unfashionable, and I am not in the least likely to change. So you see, there is very little reason for you to pursue a course that must prove exceedingly ill-advised in the end."

Absorbed in pointing out the illogic of her abductor's thinking, Francie failed to note that the earl had pulled up on the reins or that the curricle was coming to a decided halt, until without warning she found herself confronted by a Ransome, who far from displaying any signs of a demented state, appeared remarkably clear-headed.

"What course I pursue, my love, has, I fear, very little to do with reason," replied Harry, impaling her with eyes like steely points of flame. "If it did, you may be certain I should have given in long ago to the temptation to throttle you. But then love, I have found, is seldom subject to the rules of logic. You will marry me, Francine Elizabeth Powell, across the anvil if necessary, precisely *because* you are stubborn, hard-headed, and hopelessly unfashionable. I have come to the realization it is the only way I shall ever convince you that I am in earnest pursuit of you and have been since that ill-fated night in that cursed inn when you hurtled yourself into my arms and commanded me to kiss you. Why else do you think I should have been persuaded to break every canon of a gentleman, even going so far as to introduce a gently born female into a gaming house, not to mention a brothel? I believe I have been patient, Francie, but even I have my limits."

Francie, considerably startled by his vehemence, not to mention the fact that he had wrapped the reins about the brake and was moving toward her on the seat with a look of stern purpose on his handsome face, drew back in alarm.

"But, Ransome, only think what you are inviting," she said, attempting once more to break through to his rational mind. "No matter how much I should wish to make you a conformable wife, I am by my very nature doomed to fail. I shall undoubtedly succumb to irresistible impulse."

Far from being discouraged at such a prospect, Harry moved to clasp her in a ruthless embrace. "I have no doubt of it. I am in fact counting on it," he informed her. "It is one of the things that I find most attractive in you. I daresay I shall never be bored with you as my wife."

"No, we shall undoubtedly find ourselves plunged into one bumblebroth after another," Francie agreed, thinking that he had indeed abandoned all sense of reason. "You, after all, have already demonstrated that you cannot overcome your highly developed sense of honor. You broke your word to me. You swore you would not fight for me."

"On the contrary, my dear," replied Harry, distracting his impossible love by nibbling at her exposed ear. "I swore I should not engage in a duel over a female for whom I could not possibly care. Clearly, you failed to make the pertinent distinction."

Francie, who in spite of her extensive study of Philidor, was beginning to realize she was no match for Ransome at games of strategy, tried once more to stave off the inevitable. "But, Ransome, I wish you will be sensible. If you truly cared for me, clearly you would not have disappeared after your duel with Laverly. I daresay you were obeying your first instincts for self-preservation. Indeed, I cannot conceive why you should have come after me."

"I came because your sister Florence was foresighted enough to write to me informing me that you had decided to fling away your chance at happiness. I'm afraid, my love, that I could not allow you to fling mine away, too. Having waited all my life to find the woman with whom I could happily spend the rest of my life, I have no intention of letting her slip through my fingers now. You will marry me, Francie. You really have no choice in the matter. It remains only to determine whether it will be over the anvil or in your family chapel. Though I am inclined to take your father's advice to tie the knot with dispatch, before, as it were, the filly takes the bit in her mouth and bolts from the stable, your mama, I warn you, has her heart set on a formal wedding."

Francie started, considerably taken aback at what must clearly be a delusion on his part. "But you cannot possibly know what Mama would wish. And Papa—" Suddenly stricken with realization, Francie bolted upright in the earl's arms. "Ransome, you have been to Greensward."

"It did seem the logical step," confessed Harry, taking undue advantage of her distracted state to kiss the palm of her hand. "You could not be brought to see my intentions were of a serious nature. You left me no recourse but to ask your father's permission to marry you, and for that I had to go to Greensward. Which is how, by the way, that I discovered the Phillip you insisted I saved on the Continent and with whom I was wholly unfamiliar was Lathrop. You might have saved me a deal of speculation had you seen fit to tell me the story of how Lathrop ensnared his adored Lucy."

"Oh, but I never thought," exclaimed Francie, struck with realization. "Of course you could not know Lathrop presented himself to us as Phillip Carmichael. He had overheard Lucy swear she would never marry Patrick Windholm since he could not possibly need her, save as a brood mare to bear him the requisite heir. We have all called him Phillip ever since. But if you were at Greensward, how could Flo have gotten word to you ahead of my own arrival? Indeed, Ransome, why did you come after me at all, when you might have waited for me there?"

"Because I had already returned to London. I was, in fact, preparing to come to see you, when I found Lady Florence's letter waiting for me. And, now, my impossible love, having been in pursuit of you nearly the entire length of England, not once, but twice, I am afraid I really must insist on an answer. I do not hesitate to warn you that I am in no mood for a rejection. Indeed, if you do not immediately say you will be my wife, I shall most assuredly throttle you."

"That is all very fine and good, my lord," countered Francie, who, far from evincing the least trepidation in the face of such a threat, felt herself trembling on the brink of happiness. "But you still have not told me *why* you have determined on what is clearly an irrational course. Perhaps it is only that insanity runs in your family. In which case, I should feel obligated to save you from making a dreadful mistake by turning down your proposal of marriage."

"Impudent brat," Harry growled, clasping her savagely to his chest. "Your only obligation is to save yourself from a fate worse than death. Why the devil do you think I should have done it? I love you, Francie Powell. And do not think that I have not questioned my sanity any number of times these past weeks. I haven't the least doubt that I am mad. I shall undoubtedly continue in such a state until I have reached a very advanced age and all because I had the misfortune to fall victim to a roguish imp of a girl who is prone to cataclysmic misadventure. Say you will marry me, Francie, or I shall not be held responsible for the consequences."

"In that case, my lord, clearly I have no choice in the matter. I haven't the least wish to contribute further to your delicate mental balance." Flinging her arms about his neck, Francie lifted a glowing face to his. "Oh, yes, my dearest Harry. I will marry you. I love you far too much to wish ever to live without you. Besides, I could never resist a challenge. I daresay, together, we shall have the most glorious grand adventure."

Epilogue

It was the end of June. The tower room at Lathrop brooded in the late afternoon sunlight, stark and grey. Its thick stone walls, radiating narrow arched windows, admitted only a feeble light, which served more to add to the atmosphere of gloom rather than to dispel it. The Earl of Bancroft's four daughters, seated on colorful quilts spread on the floor, their lovely faces lit by the glow of a lantern, hardly noticed, however. They were listening in rapt attention as Francie related the tale of her adventures.

"You did what?" Florence, considerably startled, was moved to exclaim at one point.

"I rode in the Quorn country," repeated Francie, her blue eyes gleaming with remembered excitement. "You should have seen Jester. We came to a double oxer with a pool of water on the off-side. Jester never balked. He took it like a veteran. Oh, it was marvelous. The pack was all around us, and the huntsmen were strewn out behind, save for Ransome. He was with the lead hounds at the front. I was never so taken aback as when I looked up to see him, halted on a hill, watching me." Francie flushed all over again at the memory.

"He was magnificent, but so odiously arrogant. He actually had the gall to salute me with his quirt. Naturally, I did not know then who he was. If I had, I should have been saved a deal of worry. I should have known at once that my name and reputation were safe in his care."

"You never told me any of this," Flo said reprovingly.

"If I had, you would have sent me home before my first tea party. You know you would have done," Francie retorted, screwing her face up into a comical frown, then immediately she was off again on a new tangent. "Only wait, Lucy, until you see Ransome's hunter, Brutus. He is a great, rangy beast. You will think him ugly until you see him run. Ransome insists he is too big for my weight, but all the same I intend to have him as soon as we are married next week."

"Francie, for shame," laughed Lucy. "Poor Harry. I daresay before you are through, you will not leave him a horse to call his own."

"And I think you underestimate Harry," interjected Josephine with a knowing smile. "From what I have seen, I think Francie has met her match at last, and in more ways than one."

"Pooh." Francie gave a toss of her head. "I have every intention of giving Harry a run for his money. He has assured me, after all, that he depends on me to make certain he is never bored. It is practically my duty to keep him off his balance."

Florence threw up her hands in horror. "Good Lord, the man does not know what he has let himself in for. No one in his right mind who knew Francie would issue her a license for mayhem."

"Yes, but then he is not in his right mind. That is what I love most about him," Francie said, her face glowing. "I daresay there is not another man alive who would take me to a gaming house, let alone a bordello masquerading as a boarding house for itinerant actresses. And who, but Harry, would be intimately acquainted with a notorious highwayman who, besides having carrot red hair, stands little taller than a new born foal?"

"Who would have thought," said Josephine whimsically, "that all those chess lessons with Papa would turn out to be useful one day?"

"Only Francie would have forgotten a purse of a hundred pounds in the heat of excitement over winning the match," chuckled Lucy fondly. "And only Francie would find herself dressed up in a Paphian's clothing waiting to bludgeon her first caller with a pink parasol. Really, Francie, you must sit down with me and describe every detail of the house and the people. And Laughing Jack Cates. I must hear all about him. He sounds a perfectly marvelous character for one of my stories."

"I found Mr. Cates to be quite agreeable," Florence interjected a trifle defensively. "And he did help save Paul's life, not once, but twice, not to mention Francie's and mine. I daresay there is a deal more to Mr. Cates than meets the eye."

"Indeed there is," grinned Francie. "As it happens, he designed and made up the dress I am wearing."

"No, I do not believe you," exclaimed Florence,

who had earlier admired the sprigged muslin with the gay flounce around the hem.

"Clearly, you are bamming us," Lucy appended, eyeing her younger sister with a gleaming eye.

"Nevertheless, it is perfectly true," Francie assured them. "It seems Laughing Jack was never all that successful as a highwayman. No one ever took him seriously. Well, after all, who could, when he would give into the giggles whenever he tried to practice his profession? And he was far too good spirited ever to wish to shoot someone simply for the purpose of demonstrating he was actually perfectly serious."

"I should think he was operating under extreme disadvantages," gurgled Josephine, hugging her knees to her chest with delight at such an absurdity.

"The thing was, he had yet to find his true calling," Francie informed them. "That did not come until he had a cart loaded with bolts of crimson satin practically dumped in his lap. Not knowing what else to do with his booty, he set about making dresses, which he sold for a modest sum to the ladies of his acquaintance on Swallow Street. The Scarlet Women of Swallow Street are practically famous. Which was how Harry was able to interest a certain costumier, who had been of service to him on more than one occasion, in buying Jack's creations. You see before you a Jacques Catier Original. The French anonym was Harry's idea. He thought, besides protecting the costumier from the possibility of adverse publicity, it would lend Jack a certain cachet."

"How very clever of Harry," Lucy exclaimed, green glints of laughter dancing in her remarkable eyes.

"On the other hand, I should think it would be a deal more entertaining to tell people I was wearing a dress designed by a formerly notorious highwayman who began his dress-making career by garbing the muslin set of Swallow Street in scarlet. I daresay Jack would be the rage overnight with such a story."

"Lucy!" Florence objected, sending a pointed glance at Josephine. "That is hardly a topic for delicately bred females."

"You mean children, do you not?" Josephine interjected with a wry grimace. "I'm afraid it is far too late to keep me in ignorance now, Flo. Daisy told me all about Jack Cates and the Scarlet Women of Swallow Street. Besides, I have known about the muslin set for simply ages. I have read all of Lucy's books, after all."

"But of course she has, Flo," Lucy said, exchanging a twinkling glance with her youngest sister Jo. "We have all learned about them at one time or another. It is simply one of those absurdities that delicately bred women are supposed to know nothing about such things. What dull creatures we must be if we were as innocent as such silly precepts would have us."

Josephine, visibly expanding at being accepted on an equal footing with her older sisters, was moved to declare, "Daisy confided in me that Jack's new enterprise has enabled him to engage the Scarlet Women of Swallow Street in more gainful employment. Nearly a score of them are now working for him as seamstresses and in other capacities. I daresay what we need are more men like Laughing Jack Cates."

"Certainly we could do with fewer like Ralph and Dinkerly Dan," Francie observed darkly. "Not to mention Armstead."

"Or females like Madame Veronique Noire," added Florence, her fine eyes hardening to blue glints of anger. "Whenever I think how close she came to ending Paul's life, I find myself wishing her gladly to the devil. Indeed, I cannot find an ounce of forgiveness for what she has done, no matter what Mama says about pitying those whose lives are molded by poverty and hardship. Thank heavens Paul never actually—well, you know," she ended, unable to voice the unspeakable aloud. Blushing rosily, she ducked her head, only to lift it again with a glow of pride. "Not that he would have done. I know that now. Indeed, we have come to know one another a deal better in the past few weeks, which is why I believe Paul would not mind if I divulged our little secret to you."

"A secret. How scrumptious," exclaimed Josephine. "It is just like it used to be when we plotted how we should get even with the boys for one of their dreadful practical jokes. Please do tell us what it is, Flo."

"Indeed, Flo, out with it," Francie declared. "Pray do not keep us in suspense."

Florence, her lovely face alight with fondness for her sisters and the joy of her gladsome news, gazed around her at the others. "We were going to announce it anyway at dinner tonight, but, well, we are all here, the four of us together for the first time since Lucy married Phillip, and who knows when we shall be again? Nothing could make what I have to tell you more dear to my heart than to share it with my three sisters here and now. Only, you must promise not to give me away to Mama and Papa and the others."

"We promise!" came in an impatient chorus.

"Only, tell us before we burst," added Francie, clasping Flo's hand and giving it a shake in her eagerness.

"Very well," said Flo with an exaggerated air of importance belied by the glow of happiness in her eyes. "I had suspected it for some time, but we only made sure the day before we left London for Greensward. It is, of course, early days yet, but the doctor seemed quite positive that I am—"

"*Increasing!*" squealed Francie before Florence could get the word out. With a gleeful cry, she flung her arms about her older sister. "It is just what I hoped for you and Paul. Indeed, I could not be happier for you both!"

"Flo, how simply splendid," chimed in Lucy, hugging both Florence and Francie. Then, remembering Josephine, who was dancing about, trying to get Florence's attention, Lucy drew the youngest Powell into the joyful circle.

It was some time before the cries and excited laughter subsided, leaving the sisters huddled in a circle, their arms clasped about one another's waists, their eyes locked in awareness of the specialness of the moment.

"I wish it could always be like this," sighed Jo, voicing the sentiment that was in each of their hearts.

"The four of us together. And the boys and Mama and Papa. Why does everything always have to change?"

Francie's heart went out to Josephine, who was soon to be the last Powell hopefully left at Greensward. Their papa had purchased the twins their colors, and William had determined to set up in bachelor's quarters in London for a year to obtain what his papa called Town Bronze. Immediately, after the wedding on Sunday, Francie and Harry were to leave for a honeymoon tour of Scotland, while Florence and Paul were to take up residence at Oaks, the family estate in Devonshire. Even though Lucy would be within easy access at Lathrop, Francie could not but be aware Josephine must have been feeling rather left out of late. At fourteen, the four years until she would be of an age to follow in her sisters' footsteps must seem to stretch out like an eternity before Josephine.

Still, the glorious adventure that had befallen each and every one of the older girls still awaited the youngest of the Powell hopefuls. Francie rejoiced in the knowledge that Josephine had yet to experience all the delectable uncertainties and ultimate discoveries that went along with living life to the fullest. There was, after all, a great deal to rejoice in at being a woman, she reflected, smiling happily to herself at the thought of Ransome, who was everything she could ever have hoped for in a husband. One day Josephine would know for herself that change was in truth only the spice of life, the thing that made every new day, along with the old, something to cherish. It was, after all, the stuff that memories were made of, she thought, storing up in her mind this most special of moments, which, with all the others before and ahead, would be the sum of her life. She meant to make sure that that life was rich with experiences.

"Pray don't be such a gaby, Jo," Francie said at last. "Some things never change. We shall always be sisters, and, even if we are parted, we shall always have with us the memories of Greensward."

ABOUT THE AUTHOR

Sara Blayne lives with her family in Portales, New Mexico. She is the author of eight Zebra regency romances and is currently working on her ninth, which will be published in June 1998. Sara loves hearing from her readers and you may write to her c/o Zebra Books. Please include a sell-addressed, stamped envelope if you wish a response.

WATCH FOR THESE ZEBRA REGENCIES

LADY STEPHANIE   (0-8217-5341-X, $4.50)
by Jeanne Savery
Lady Stephanie Morris has only one true love: the family estate she
has managed ever since her mother died. But then Lord Anthony Rider
arrives on her estate, claiming he has plans for both the land and the
woman. Stephanie soon realizes she's fallen in love with a man whose
sensual caresses will plunge her into a world of peril and intrigue . . . a
man as dangerous as he is irresistible.

BRIGHTON BEAUTY   (0-8217-5340-1, $4.50)
by Marilyn Clay
Chelsea Grant, pretty and poor, naively takes school friend Alayna
Marchmont's place and spends a month in the country. The devastating
man had sailed from Honduras to claim his promised bride, Miss
Marchmont. An affair of the heart may lead to disaster . . . unless a
resourceful Brighton beauty finds a way to stop a masquerade and
keep a lord's love.

LORD DIABLO'S DEMISE   (0-8217-5338-X, $4.50)
by Meg-Lynn Roberts
The sinfully handsome Lord Harry Glendower was a gambler and the
black sheep of his family. About to be forced into a marriage of convenience, the devilish fellow engineered his own demise, never having
dreamed that faking his death would lead him to the heavenly refuge
of spirited heiress Gwyn Morgan, the daughter of a physician.

A PERILOUS ATTRACTION   (0-8217-5339-8, $4.50)
by Dawn Aldridge Poore
Alissa Morgan is stunned when a frantic passenger thrusts her baby
into Alissa's arms and flees, having heard rumors that a notorious
highwayman posed a threat to their coach. Handsome stranger Hugh
Sebastian secretly possesses the treasured necklace the highwayman
seeks and volunteers to pose as Alissa's husband to save her reputation.
With a lost baby and missing necklace in their care, the couple embarks
on a journey into peril—and passion.

*Available wherever paperbacks are sold, or order direct from the
Publisher. Send cover price plus 50¢ per copy for mailing and
handling to Penguin USA, P.O. Box 999, c/o Dept. 17109,
Bergenfield, NJ 07621. Residents of New York and Tennessee must
include sales tax. DO NOT SEND CASH.*

LOOK FOR THESE REGENCY ROMANCES

WATCH FOR THESE REGENCY ROMANCES

ROMANCE FROM FERN MICHAELS

DEAR EMILY   (0-8217-4952-8, $5.99)

WISH LIST   (0-8217-5228-6, $6.99)

AND IN HARDCOVER:

VEGAS RICH   (1-57566-057-1, $25.00)